FITTING IN Is Hard To Do

Semester 1

WESTBROOK HIGH SERIES

A novel by

HEAVEN J. FOX

Fitting In (Is Hard to Do) Book 1 Semester 1

Fox E. Flinn Books

First Edition Printing: September 2014

ISBN-13: 978-1503006096
ISBN-10: 1503006093

Website: www.foxeflinn.com

Twitter: @heavenjfox

Website: http://www.heavenjfox.foxeflinn.com/

Fan page: https://www.facebook.com/YAHeavenJ/

DEDICATION

Dedicated to my entire family. I would not have been able to even write a single word on paper if it weren't for you guys pushing and uplifting me!.

ACKNOWLEDGMENTS

First and foremost, Thank You, Lord for giving me the gift of storytelling. Please continue giving me the words to reach out and teach someone. If it had not been for You… I don't know where I'd be.
Thanks to my Mom, my husband, all my children, my sisters and brothers, nieces, nephews, and grandkids for being there for me.
Last but not least a very special Thanks to all my readers.

1 CHAPTER ONE

The most basic human desire is to feel like you belong. Fitting in is important.
~Simon Sinek

AMBER STYLES LOOKED IN the mirror at her fifteen-year-old body and detested it. She wanted her size 2 jeans to be at least a size 10-12, so she can have one of those "Apple bottom booties" like the girls in her class. They got so much attention from guys. She too wanted that attention. She wanted a guy… any guy, to walk past her in the hallway and feel her booty so she could slap him across the head and tell him to quit playing!

Amber wrapped a few pieces of toilet paper around her hand and stuffed it into each sides of her bra. She cupped each breast with her palm and gave them a few squeezes hoping the toilet paper wouldn't look so lumpy. She maneuvered it around a few times so that she could acquire a more natural looking roundness. Bending down in front of her full-length mirror, she used her arms to squeeze whatever bosoms she had together. *What does a chick have to do to get some cleavage?* She questioned herself.

"Ew, that's disgusting! Is that what you girls really do?" Cam'Ron says as he burst into his sister's room.

"Cam, Get out!" Amber screams as she snatches the toilet paper from her bosom and throws them in the wastebasket.

Cam'Ron didn't bulge an inch. Instead he says, "Give me $5 and I won't tell Roman Davis."

"Ugh! You know I don't have $5!"

"Ok, suit yourself."

Amber reaches into her pants pockets. "Here! All I have is $2. Take it and shut up."

♥♥♥

Amber and her two best friends, Willow and Ryder, climbed into the school bus. Since Willow and Ryder boarded first, they filled the first empty seat in the front, which left Amber alone to search for a seat herself.

Amber's eyes shifted toward the back as she saw Symphony, a sophomore, halfway standing and waving. "Come back here with us."

Amber's heart sank into her stomach and chills radiated down her spine. *Could Symphony Perkins be talking to her?* Amber smiled and waved back about to make her way to the back of the bus to sit with all the cool and popular kids until she saw Symphony's face distorted as if she smelled something funky.

"Excuse me." Spirit Sweet said as she maneuvered her way around Amber. She was now embarrassed. How could she have been so stupid to think that someone like Symphony would actually smile, wave, and tell her to come to the back with her.

Amber just sat in the first seat she saw next to a random girl. "Uhn unn… this seat is taken!" The girl pushes on Amber to move out of the seat. Not wanting to draw any more attention to herself, she quickly got up and sat somewhere else. That was it. Amber thought to herself, tomorrow she will make sure she gets on the bus before Willow or Ryder and make one of them have to find a suitable seat.

"This is some bull!" Quincy Garnett boards the bus and head towards the back. I see they back on this mess again!"

"Bruh, what are you hollin' about now?" Roman Davis laughed as he got up so Quincy can scoot over to the window. "It's way too early in the morning for all that."

"I'm just saying it lame as heck that the bus passes us to go pick up the high-rollers in the condos and then roll back down the hill and pick us up last." Quincy shakes his head. "This bus full to the max already can't find a seat."

"Well, you know they have to pick the queen up first." Symphony looked over at Quincy and shined her bright smile in his face.

Spirit laughed. "You should be smart like me and at least walk up to the next bus stop."

"You need to walk up to the condo's with yo fat ass." Quincy shot a look at Spirit that dared her to keep it going because the way that he was feeling right now, he can crack jokes all day.

"Aight! Y'all calm down and chill." Roman looks over at Quincy. "I don't know what your problem is, I saved you a seat." Roman laughs because he knows Quincy hates sitting on the inside.

"Nigga! If you were really doing me a favor, you'd let me sit where you are. I'm taller than you anyways,"

"You wish!" Roman sat back and looked over at Symphony and licked his lips. "Tell ya girl to trade me seats so this nigga can stop crying."

Hunter Santos sighs as she get up to change seats. "I really don't care where I sit as long as y'all can shut up." She nestles in by the window seat and closes her eyes.

"What?" Roman waited for Symphony to slide in the seat first.

"Unh unh…. This is my seat. You are sitting with me, so in ya go boo boo!"

"Aw man, you have got to be kidding me!" Roman scoots in the seat and sits by the window. "I'm supposed to be your man that means the woman gets the window and the man is always supposed to be on the outside."

"Says who?" Symphony wanted to know.

Quincy on the other hand stretched his long legs in the isle and laughed at Roman. "So what that made me when the shoe was on the other foot?"

2 CHAPTER TWO
AMBER STYLES
Crooked Smile

MY MEDIUM COMPLEXION SKIN tone would have been perfect if it wasn't for the 1001 darks spots that had taken over. I knew I wasn't the finest thing on this earth but I also knew I wasn't the ugliest. If I could get rid of some of these cosmetic defects, I might just be considered desirable to boys.

I stand in front of the bathroom mirror fussing with my two-week old relaxed hair. It was broken off in some areas but those parts were easy to cover with the longer strands that adorned my head. I part my hair on the side and flat iron my 'barely to the bottom of my ear' length hair straight down and bump the ends, but not too much to give my hair the appearance of being longer than it really was.

I thought about the girls at school and how they all seemed to have long, bouncy, silky hair. It might not have been theirs but they owned it in so many ways. "They're mothers take them to the shop." I mumble aloud. I hate the way I look and having to get my relaxer from a Dark & Lovely box, done in Joi's Kitchen & Kurls. My mother's kitchen.

The way my skin feels right now, I can't wait to get out of these clothes. As I ran my bath water, I talked to my girl Willow on the phone. "What are you doing best friend?" Willow asked me.

"Pouring vinegar, kosher salt, and olive oil in my bathwater."

"What? Are you trying to make yourself a salad?" Willow bust out laughing as if she'd made the funniest joke in the world. Willow and me, go way back to elementary and practically did everything together. Where you saw one, you would see the other.

"Anyway, best friend you ready for tomorrow?" Willow asked me over the phone.

"You know I am!" I looked into the bathroom mirror again, imagining the way I wanted to look tomorrow. From what I imagine makes me smile, but my smile quickly diminishes when I see my two front teeth staring back at me. Taunting me. It was as if they were laughing and making fun of me too. They were bigger than most and weren't as straight as everyone else's but if I smile just right, it wouldn't be noticeable. A lot of times people think I'm mad because I don't smile a lot. Whatever. If they had these things, they wouldn't find much to smile about either.

"Amber! Did you hear me?" Willow screams into the phone for the umpteenth time.

"Nah, what you say?" I was too busy thinking about my imperfections and forgot all about my friend on the phone.

"Never mind." Willow said defeated.

I turn off my almost overflowed bath water and thought of a way to console my best friend. "Aight best friend, go head. I couldn't hear with this water running." I lie.

"I was saying –"

"Hold that thought, my dad is beeping in," I cut Willow off without waiting for her to respond. "Hey dad."

"Hey beautiful." I roll my eyes to the thought of me being compared to beauty and scratch the rashes that had formed on my neck and my arm. "I was just calling to see how you guys were doing."

"Thanks dad." I knew he wasn't calling for just me. I was about to tell my father that I'd give him a call back because Willow was on the other line but the phone click alerting me that Willow had already hung up.

"So is your Mama still seeing that guy?"

I hate when he confronted me about my mother's business. He knew darn well my mom was still seeing Keith. "Yes, daddy."

I have to sit here and babysit all his humph's and sighs over the phone as if this was the first time he'd heard all this. I could be taking my bath right now! I tilt my head and stare at the ceiling while tapping my foot because I know what's coming next. "See, if it wasn't for that dude, me and your Mama could have gotten back together. I've been sitting here waiting on your mom." He sulks some more and says, "I-I ain't seeing nobody!"

"I know daddy." I got so tired of hearing this stuff all the time. Every time I turn around… I'm always being put in the middle some kind of way. I walk into the kitchen near my mom because I knew what my father's next question would be.

"Where's your –"

"Right here." I cut him off handing the phone to my mother who wore that, 'What the hell you giving me the phone for look.' She snatches the phone from my hand but I already knew the frustration wasn't intended for me.

"Stop scratching! You're making it worse!" My mom says referring to me dang near mutilating the eczema off my skin. "Go take your bath and put your cream on!"

♥♥♥

After taking my bath, I was going to give my hair another shot but Willow called me back and we got engrossed into deep conversation.

"You ain't find no cute dude that you want to hook-up with yet?" I ask her that because she rarely talk about any dudes she might like.

"Best friend, please! I got better things to do with my time than thinking about some Westbrook High boys."

"What! In a minute, I'm goin' think you play for the other team." I couldn't help but laugh out loud. "So you saying you ain't going to Winter Formal?"

"Yeah, I'm going to Winter Formal! Why do I need a dude to take me to Winter Formal when I can take myself? If bad comes to worse, you and I can just roll up in there together. Plus Amber, that is so far off from now… we just started school and you already thinking about that."

Ugh! Can this chick get any lamer? I mean, who the heck goes to Winter Formal by themselves? I be damn if I go to my first or any High School function by myself or with another chick. "This ain't no elementary or middle school dance, Willow. I suggest you start finding you a date because I know I'm gonna' find one. So yeah, I'm thinking about it now 'cause I need to find me a date."

"Yeah okay! Who? I know not Roman Davis?"

"Why not Roman Davis?"

"Well, a couple of reasons actually. For one, he's not on your level. For two, I think he's seeing Symphony Perkins."

"He is seeing Symphony Perkins… I'm in middle school and even I know that, Amber!"

"Get off the phone Cam'Ron! Ugh!!!"

"Hiiiii, Willoooow." My brother sings into the phone ignoring anything I said.

"Heeeey, Cam! "Willow sings back, "Now get off the phone… we girl-talkin'."

"Ok." Just like that, he hangs up. Just to be 100% sure, he hung up, I click over to the other line to make sure I hear the 3-way dial tone. I continue on…

"You know what? Your name should be Willow Killjoy Martin. You always gotta' hate and put somebody down." Even though she was my best friend, emotionally it seemed like she never had my back.

"Amber please! You know they are on a different level than us. They're sophomores and popular as heck. When have we ever hung out with a squad? Have you ever been friends with a cheerleader? Or dated someone that was on the basketball or football team? I'll answer for you.... No! Because neither have I. It's always been us three musketeers."

Willow was referring to her, me, and Ryder. We've been 3-deep since elementary. It wasn't like we met and formed an unending bond, we were more or less thrown together from being outcast from the nerds and the popular group. We weren't athletic enough to be popular or smart enough to be nerds. We were nothing! I'm tired of being nothing and a nobody. Willow and Ryder might be content with that, but not me!

I even thought that since we were all in the same church with different kids other than the ones we went to school with, that it would be different. I thought that at church, nobody would judge me or look down on me. That it would be an automatic common bond. I found out real quick that going to church was just as stressful as going to school. I still had to deal with funky attitudes, snobby-ness, judgment, and cliques. We "Three musketeers" will always be the outcast no matter where we were. That's why it is so important for me to change the curse that's plagued me all my life. I was more determined than ever to do whatever I had to do to be popular and accepted by the other side.

Any smile I had when we first started this conversation had been long gone. Willow was definitely a fun-killer. The least she could have done was to humor me and let me have some fun with my fantasies. I knew that most of the stuff I said and talked about was only wishful thinking. But dang, if she was supposed to be my best friend she should have joined in and had some fun right along with me. Willow's mind-numbing attitude had me fuming.

"Amber!" My mom yells for me.

"Huh!" I answer back irritated placing my hand over the receiver so I wouldn't scream in Willow's ear.

"Don't huh me... You better come when I call you!" Ugh! I wish she would make up her mind on what she wants me to do. When I don't say nothing and just come, she yells at me to say something.

"All right best friend," I said in my normal tone trying not to show Willow how annoyed she had made me. "I'm 'bout to go see what my mom wants and finish my hair for tomorrow.

Willow didn't even notice how my mood had changed. "All right best friend, lata."

I was so annoyed I didn't even say good-bye, I just hung up the phone.

♥♥♥

BAM! BAM! BAM!

"Who at the door?" My mom yells. She was in the kitchen trying to piece something together because it was the end of the month and food was scarce.

My thirteen-year-old brother Cam'Ron wizzes past me, runs into his room, and slam the door behind him.

"You could have gotten the door!" I holler at him but it bounces off his bedroom door and comes back to me void.

I pull open the front door and it's another angry mother holding the hand of her O-So-Precious child who could never do any wrong in her eyes. "Where's your mother!" The slightly overweight woman throws at me along with a whiff of cigarette breath smelling like she brushed her teeth with a whole pack of cigarettes. Her hair is standing every which way on her head as if she had just gotten off the couch from watching her stories. She blows her cigarette smoke through the screen and it smacks me in the face.

"Ma!" I summon my mother feeling sorry for the unsuspecting soul on the other end of the screen door.

"What!"

"Somebody wants you!"

"Who the hell is it?"

How the heck was I supposed to know? I look at the woman and she's obviously fuming. I don't know if she was blowing smoke from her nose or if it were coming from the top of her head. "I don't know!" I yell back, never having seen this woman before in my life.

Within a few seconds, my mother comes storming from the kitchen. She knew as well as I did what was up when she saw the lady and her son standing there with a bloody nose.

"Your son punched my son in the nose and made it bleed!"

My mom shifted her weight onto one foot and placed her hand on her hip. "Cam'Ron!" She yells without taking her eyes off the woman on the other side of the screen door.

My brother opens his bedroom door and peer out. "Yes?" My mom turns around and looks at Cam'Ron as if he already knew what she wanted.

"Is that him?" Mz. Ghetto Fab asked her son. He nods his head the best he could while holding the toilet paper to his nose.

"Did you do that?" My mom turns around and questions my brother.

"Okay… wait… see… what happened was—"

WHOMP! My mom smacks Cam'Ron across the back of the head. "Mommy… wait… you didn't let me explain…" Cam'Ron and the boy began to go back and forth about each other's versions of what happened. Of course each version was to make each of them look like innocent bystanders.

Having enough, my mom said, "Well we are getting nowhere. I'll keep my son over this way and maybe you should do the same with yours." My mother had had enough of the shenanigans.

"Don't tell me what to do with my child!"

My mom throws her hand on her hip and cocks her head to the side, "Okay, then what do you suggest?" My mom asks sarcastically. "Would you like me to pop my son in the nose so he could bleed too?"

"What I want is for someone to pay for this shirt!"

"For what? You need me to wash it for you?"

"This is a AKOO shirt!" My mom looks at the woman as if she's speaking a foreign language. "I paid $80.00 for this damn shirt and you goin' give me my money!"

My mom gasps and no longer can she compose herself because she thought this lady was on drugs.

"Trick please! You need to spend that money on fighting lesson because clearly your son just got his ass kicked in his "AKOO" shirt!" My mother slams the door in the woman's face and leaves her out there screaming and yelling at the door.

My mom raises her hands toward the ceiling, "Lord, Jesus give me patience because if you give me strength, I'm going to need bail money too!" She looks at Cam'Ron and says, "Get your butt in your room until I tell you to come out. You goin' make sure they throw us out on the street. Everyday someone complaining about you! Don't go back outside!"

♥♥♥

I look at my hair in the mirror and compare it to Symphony and the other girls. "Ugh!" I pick up my pink Bristol brush and start hitting myself in the head. I pull and yank at each ugly strand on my head until it's a big bushy mess. "I hate you!" I shriek at my hair in the mirror.

"What's wrong?" My mother, Joi, says as she peek her head into the bathroom.

"Nothing." I still hold a frown with evil eyes and stare at my reflection in the mirror.

"Awww baby, it's alright. Here let me help you." My mother grabs the comb and began to flat iron my hair. The more my mom touches my hair, the more enrage I become. When my mom finishes, she pats my hair to poof it with her hands. I hate when she does this, my hair now remained above my ears.

"Stop!" I move my head so my mom couldn't touch it anymore and run into my room to place a scarf over it to cover the bigger mess she made.

"What is the matter with you?" My mom's face bore worry and concern for me.

Knowing that my mom wouldn't understand, I just say, "Nothing." I know it's a lie but I didn't want to hurt my mother's feelings with the truth.

Not letting up, she persists until I give her an answer.

"Why can't I get weave?"

"Why would you want weave? Your only 15 years old and your hair is beautiful."

I jump up and run to my dresser mirror. "Where!" I rip the scarf from my head. "You tell me where?!"

I knew I had gone too far but it was too late to take it back now. My mom took a step back to readjust her thoughts because clearly this was not her daughter standing before her. "For one." My mom paused holding up her index finger. "You need to slow ya roll because you are getting a little too fly at the mouth!" She folds her arms across her chest. "Where do you think you get off talking to me like that? Don't think you're too big for me to grab a belt and whoop yo ass, because I will!"

I knew my mother spoke the truth so I put my attitude and mouth in check real quick. "Ma, I just can't stand my hair. All the other girls at school go to the shop and wear weave."

"Since when have I raised you to be just like all the other girls?" I remain silent because I knew I was fighting a losing battle. "I know that Willow don't go to no shop, nor do she wear weave."

"Aw c'mon Ma! That's different and you know it! Willow has nice hair." I began to feel a twinge of jealousy tugging on my insides.

Feeling agitated, my mom shook her head, "Unh uh… I'm not going to sit up here and do a roundabout when I already told you no!" My mom glares at me from above the rim of her glasses. "Now wash your hands and dust all that hair off you so we can eat.

3 CHAPTER THREE

Live your dream beneath your passion and stand with your team… Cheerleading may not be your life, but it's mine!

AMBER'S MOTHER TELLS HER to go find, Cam'Ron. He was supposed to have been in the house. Better yet, he shouldn't have been outside playing. After dinner, he was to take the trash to the dumpster and come right back. He never listens. Amber hoped she didn't see anybody from school. Her mother had her out there looking for him and looking like a fool. She had on her pajama pants and headscarf. Amber wasn't about to take it off and have to go through all that to put it back on again.

Amber walked on the far side of the parking lot and held her head down because she saw Symphony Perkins with her cheerleading squad practicing in the parking lot. She sure didn't want them to see her. Especially not looking like this. She wanted to look. Wished she could go over and join in but she was too shy to be somebody's cheerleader. "Bring it on" was one of her favorite movies.

Push 'em back!
Push 'em back!
Way Ba—

Symphony grabs her purse she sat on top of some random person's car and checked the time on her cell. It read 6:53pm. "Excuse me!" Her WestPoint squad stopped cheering as they directed their attention to a 180 pound, Spirit Sweet, approaching the line.

"What?" Spirit said still chomping and picking meat from a bone.

"What? I said to meet me out here at 6:00pm and you walking yo fat ass up here over an hour late, that's what!"

"Girl, my bad… I had to eat first."

"Oh, really? What you eat?"

"Girl, I had pork chops, mac & cheese, green beans, and cornbread! Oh, and washed it down with some cherry Kool-Aid!"

Symphony walk up to Spirit, "Can I have some?"

"Yeah, you can have it, it was my third piece anyway."

Symphony took the pork chop and threw it as far and hard as she could. "All I heard you say was sugar, grease, and cheese!"

♥♥♥

"Hey!" Amber stops some of her brother's friend's bike riding past her. "Have you guys seen Cam'Ron?"

"Nope."

"Alright. If you see him—"

Laughter rang out from the group of boys as Amber's head began to sting. "What was that?"

The boy looks down at the piece of meat lying on the sidewalk. "Daaaaang! Is that a pork chop?" They all bust out laughing and pointing at Amber as they rode away. Amber kicks the stupid piece of meat into the parking lot and takes a short cut walking through some of the houses hoping that Symphony and her friends weren't having a field day at her expense like the little boys.

♥♥♥

Spirit rolls her eyes at Symphony and smacks her lips. By now, the other girls were leaning on cars and sitting on the curb watching Symphony and Spirit. Symphony heard a few of them talking smack wondering how Spirit got on the team in the first place. Another girl answered because Symphony was team captain and Spirit was her friend. That may have been the case, but truth be told, Spirit can lift that 180 pounds into the air and do a mean Hercules and a split like nobody's business. By now, they all had pissed Symphony off so she told them to run two laps around the whole complexes.

"Two laps! Do you know how big these complexes are? Keyniesha asks. Symphony looks the girl up and down because she should have known better than to question her. They all take off running with mad looks on their faces.

Symphony sits on the bench at the park because it's the best spot to see the girls when they all pass around again without taking any short cuts. Even though Symphony has on her booty cut cheer shorts she crosses her legs as she sits because that's what a lady does.

The part of the bench where Symphony sits lifts a little and startles her. She looks to her left and it was Spirit sitting next to her. "Um, that definitely goes for you too!" Symphony looks Spirit up and down. "Especially you!"

"I didn't want to be on the team no way. Don't forget you asked me."

Symphony lights a Newport and blows the smoke into the air. Spirit was starting to annoy Symphony. Here she was trying to be a good friend and help Spirit lose some weight and have fun and she couldn't even take it seriously.

"How come you ain't running? Better yet, why you always talk this healthy exercise stuff and you smoke like a chimney stack?"

"Spirit, don't start with me." Symphony takes a puff and flicks the ashes onto the ground."

"Girl! Can you believe Hunter is finally back?" Spirit perches her knee onto the bench and turns her body towards Symphony. She was getting too comfortable so Symphony knew Spirit was about to get into full gossip mode.

"Yes, Spirit. I can believe it. I knew she was coming back because the only reason she left was to take care of her grandmother while she was on her sick bed."

"Yeah I know, but her mom… what's up with that?" Spirit twists her lips. "Ain't she a little too old to be having a baby?"

Symphony backs away from Spirit and looks at her as if she was losing it. *She must be having gossip withdrawal, trying to gossip about grown folks. I could care less about anyone's business who wasn't in my age range.* Symphony thought.

"Go! Run! Now!" Symphony yells and points her in the direction she should be going.

Jaylen, Quincy, and Roman walk up to where Symphony and Spirit were sitting. "C'mon bae, I'll run with you." Jaylen said. He and Roman were cousin who lived together with their grandmother. Spirit and Jaylen take off running very slow with stops in between before they even make it to the corner.

"You swingin' through right quick?" Roman asks Symphony. Symphony just looks at him, takes another puff from the cigarette, and hand it over to Quincy.

"Maybe."

"What kind of answer is maybe? Either you is or you ain't."

"It's my answer… take it or leave it."

Some girl walks through looking a hot mess. She has a scarf on her head and her face was screaming for concealer. "Hi, Symphony." Symphony jerks back and look at the guys because she knows that girl didn't just speak to her like she knew her. Symphony ignores the girl as if she never opened her mouth to say anything.

Amber has been walking around looking for Cam'Ron for at least a good 15 minutes and starts backtracking to where she thinks he might be and goes through the yellow park to see if he's there but instead she see Symphony, Roman, and Quincy. She speak to Symphony but guesses Symphony didn't hear her because she didn't say a word.

"Ah, shoot! Look at Symphony makin' new friends!" Quincy jokes and stomps out the cigarette butt on the ground.

"Boy bye!" Symphony laughs, "I don't even know her!"

"Sym-phony!" Symphony turns to the sound of her mother's voice. "Here, you have to watch her for a minute, I'll be right back." Melody, Symphony's mother, releases Symphony's hair from her ponytail and fidgets with it until she fluffs it out. "Appearances Symphony… appearances."

"No… I'm busy!" Symphony pushes her mother's hand away and scoops her hair back into the ponytail.

"It is not going to hurt you to watch your sister for a minute! You are not doing anything but talking to these little nappy-headed boys anyway!" Quincy laughs, grabs one of his baby dreads, and began to twist while Roman runs his palms across his waves.

"No… I got something to do!"

"Okay, that's fine… remember that next time you want something!" Symphony's mother takes Harmony to the swing and begin pushing her. "Weee! Higher, mommy higher!" Symphony hears Harmony say.

Symphony directs her attention back to the guys. "I'll be over after I have these girls finish their laps." Roman smiles one of his biggest smiles because he knows what's up.

"Push me! Sym-phony! Push me!" Symphony looks over towards the swing and Harmony's swing is at a standstill.

"O, hell no!" Symphony looks around the park for her mother and she's nowhere to be found. "Ooooo!" Symphony growls as she stomps over to the swings to push Harmony.

"I guess there goes our plans, huh?" Symphony doesn't answer she just keep pushing. "Ay, yo Q, man… you wanna babysit?"

"Hell no! He ain't watching my lil sister!"

"I wasn't goin' do it noway!"

"I know you wasn't! Harmony hops off the swing to run around the park with her friend.

♥♥♥

Amber stops by Willow's so she can walk around with her. Of course, Amber feels Willow always has to one-up her. Here she was in her pajamas and Willow's lounging in her, as she calls it, "house-shorts" with a red tank top with nothing but cleavage showing. Amber's A-cups aren't even big enough for all that. Willow's hair is never out of place. Its long and bra strap length. She wears it parted on the side and only gets a perm if she's tired of wearing it curly. Let her tell it, she's not mixed with anything. Says it's because she has Indian in her family. *Don't we all?* Amber thought.

At this point, Amber could care less about where Cam'Ron is. She just wants to walk back around and see if she can catch another glimpse of Roman. She didn't want him to see her though.

"So anyway…" Amber begins. "We need to talk to Sis. Jackie and see if we can start doing some praise dances to Kirk Franklin's joints.

"Geesh, Amber." Willow rolls her eyes.

"What?"

"Don't say joint and you talking about church and gospel."

Amber sucks her teeth, "Willow please! It ain't like I was talking about weed."

"Yeah, but still…" Amber waves her off because Willow's talking foolishness. "Ms. Jackie is going to say no because the Mothers of the church thinks it's too worldly.

"That's stupid! Kirk Franklin is Gospel!" Amber says as Willow shrugs her shoulders as if saying, O well."

Amber tries to change the subject. "I saw Symphony'em practicing in the parking lot."

"So… she always be out there practicing."

"So, I'm just saying don't you ever wish we were cheerleaders or a part of something big and important?"

"We are! The marching band is important." Willow scrunches her eyebrows together as if Amber was stupid for not thinking like her. "We entertain just like the cheerleaders and football players."

"Willow, please! I ain't never hear nobody giving props to the band! Well maybe, Billy, because he plays the drums. But ain't nobody ever came up to me and pat me on the back and tell me I played the mess out of that flute! Have they with your saxophone?"

"No… and I don't care!" Willow laughs a little and continues. "I don't play my sax for no one but me. I don't need nobody's pats on the backs or good jobs! I carry enough of them within myself."

♥♥♥

Symphony kept eyeing a black car that sat across the opposite side of the street. The windows were illegally tinted black so she couldn't see who was inside. At first, she didn't pay it too much attention because she thought maybe they were going to the mailboxes. Who just sits there at a little kid park and watch? All kinds of bells and whistles began to go off in Symphony's head. "Harmony!" Symphony calls to her sister. "Let's go!" This car was giving Symphony the creeps.

"Why you leaving?" Roman grabs Symphony's hand.

"Because, it's about to get dark." The girls were starting to come around from their first lap and had another round to go.

"Y'all know whose car that is?" Quincy and Roman turn around to see which car Symphony was referring to.

"What car?" They both ask.

"The black one rig— never mind." The car had snuck off without Symphony even knowing.

"Dude, you 'noided."

"Do I look like a dude to you?" Symphony gets closer in Quincy's face.

The girls were closer now and trying to run pass Symphony huffing and puffing. "Stop! What kind of fool y'all take me for?" They all looked at Symphony as if they didn't understand the question. "I know the complexes are huge but I also know that it doesn't take this long to run around it, so y'all had to be walking and goofing off! Ya know what? Go home! We will pick it up again tomorrow."

♥♥♥

After Amber and Willow go to the black park, which is on the other side of the complex, Amber's giving up because she sees her twin nightmares, Ta'Keyla and Tanga'Rae, and decide that her search is over. She turns around faster than her heart was beating before they saw her. Too late.

"Ugh! I know this ugly ass biatch ain't walk over here to our park."

"Just keep walking, Amber." Willow says to her as if Amber is stupid enough to stop. Amber begins to wonder why the twins only decide to pick on her all the time and not Willow.

Amber keeps walking and ignores them. Like her mom says, be the bigger person and walk away. It seems that's all Amber was good at. Cam'Ron however is a different story. He ain't scared of nothing or nobody. Amber thinks he just may be a bully like the twins here following them.

The way their complex were set up, it was like three different ones in one. Up on the hill, sat the big condominiums, those were the expensive ones. They had a parking lot even though the condominiums had garages attached to them. Of course, that's where Willow stayed… Ryder and Symphony. Then you have the middle complexes. They were made up of ranch style houses and apartments. These ones looked like a regular neighborhood, a street in the middle, and houses or apartments on each side. That's where Amber stayed, Roman and Hunter. Then you have the bottom… that's where the projects are… where Amber and Willow were right now. They were located at the bottom of the hill. Hence the nickname, "The Bottom." Some of the ranch styled apartment's backyards were where the projects began. So basically, it was one way in and one way out. Quincy stays there along with the twins and Spirit. Amber wasn't exactly sure where any of them really lived because all the apartments looked alike and were so close together.

"We know you hear us! Ugly bumpy-face biatch!

Ta'Keyla runs up and pushes Amber so hard her head jerks back making her feel as though she might have whiplash. Amber turns around and Tanga'Rae punches Amber right below the eye… right on her cheekbone! Amber sees stars and flashes of light. Then the pain radiates down the side of her face. But them stars ain't the only thing Amber sees. She sees two against one and Willow's back as she high-tails it back up the hill.

"Dafuq off my sister!" Cam'Ron finally shows up and pushes Tanga'Rae to the ground and now Ta'Keyla's in his face.

"Oh, I know you ain't just put yo hands on no girl!" Ta'Keyla points her long skinny finger in Cam'Ron's face.

"Yo! You aight?" Amber's stunned. In shock. And embarrassed at the same time. Roman looks at Cam'Ron and gives him a head nod while looking at Amber for a response.

"Wait 'till I tell my brothers… they goin' whoop dat ass!" Tanga'Rae dusts herself off.

"Man, goin' with all that!" Roman interjects.

"I know you ain't talkin' if you don't hur-rup they goin' get you too!"

Amber had no idea what they meant by that. As much as she wanted to be right there in Roman's presence, her cheek was killing her and so was her ego. Amber's cheek felt like it was the size of an orange sitting on her face. She could see it too well from the corner of her left eye. Obviously it was noticeable because Roman looked at it and said, "Yeah, you goin' need to put some ice on that."

"We got it…" Cam'Ron seemed to have an attitude and Amber and Roman had no idea why. Cam'Ron pulls Amber along as if he was the big brother and she was the little sister.

4 CHAPTER FOUR
SYMPHONY PERKINS
But First Let Me Take A Selfie

I hurry and try to make it home fast because now Harmony is complaining that she has to pee really bad. I unlock the door with my key and before I enter, I stretch my arm along the living room wall and flick on the light. "Okay, Harmony come on." I flick the light on in the bathroom and keep it on even after she's done.

The sun is on its way to sleep for the night. I lock the screen door but keep the front door open. Just in case something happens and I need to grab Harmony and run out real quick. I walk past our landline and pull out my cell and call, Melody. "That real messed up how you left us, Mother!" I yell into her voicemail. "When are you coming home?" I sigh, press the end button, and fumble through the mail on the table. I gaze at Melody's bank statement. "Ten-thousand dollars!" I yell breaking Harmony's concentration from her cartoons.

"Can I have some juice?"

I grab a stool and reach up high in the cabinet to grab one of Harmony's old Sippy cups, pour her some juice, and hand it to her.

"Not in this cup! This for babies."

"What color is the sofa you're sitting on, Harmony?"

"Whipe."

"And what color is the carpet that it's sitting on?"

"It's whipe too."

"And what color is your juice?" She fills her mouth with juice, holds her head back, and opens her mouth. Juice spills from the corner of her mouth and drips onto her white Piccadilly skinny jeans. "Stop!" I make her close her mouth and gulp it all down.

"Oops!" She stares down on the splash it made on her jeans. "The juice is red, Symphony."

"Exactly! So why would you do that?" I rush her into the kitchen, toss her pants into the kitchen sink, and immerse them in cold water.

I look around our posh condo. Its' going to have to be a lot of changes around here with only ten-thousand dollars in the bank. I shake my head because I just can't believe that Melody wouldn't tell me something like that. How are we supposed to live on that? She doesn't have a job and never had as long as I've been on this earth. Everyone says we look alike. I guess we do when I really think about it, but I will never be like her. I will never depend on someone else to pay my way through life. If I get money, it's going to be because I earned it from my skills and talents.

I walk past the mirror in our walkway and I can't help but stop and stare at myself. I am one fine female, if I do say so myself. And I do say so and so does everyone else. I run the palm of my hand over my flat abs. All that running, push-ups, and sit-ups were definitely not done in vain. I grab my cell and take a quick selfie. Nice! I have to load that one as my profile pic.

I look down at our Reflection foyer table where some of my trophies and photos are and notice a folder from Chanel's Modeling Service. I open it and flip through. She also had some brochures stuck inside for beauty pageants. I know she doesn't think I'm going through all that again. I am too old nor do I have a desire for any beauty pageants right now.

I text Melody from my cell and tell her she needs to hurry home because Harmony and I were starving. Melody keeps our house looking fly. It's always neat and clean and she always cooks. Well, that is when she's home. If I don't come home in time for dinner, she'll prepare my plate and have it sitting in the microwave or on top of the stove.

My mother was a neat freak when it came to house cleaning. Her dishes never sat in the sink for long. If you ate something and there were no dishes in the sink, it was your responsibility to wash it yourself. My little sister and I could leave our rooms a mess and knew like clockwork that it will be cleaned by the time I get home. But don't get it twisted, it's not like either of us kept a dirty room or did it on purposed because we knew Melody would clean it up. Melody was not a maid and we wouldn't dare treat her as such. I always secretly wondered if my mother had a mild case of OCD.

Melody didn't have too many house rules, just give respect and you'll get it. Respect her privacy and she'll respect yours. If a door was closed, it was closed for a reason so don't even bother knocking unless it was a dying/fire emergency. My mother schooled me on sex long time ago. Her rule was, if you're going to do it, be responsible and protect yourself, your body, your heart, and don't bring no baby's home because me and the baby both would be living on the street.

On my16th birthday, my mother was so happy that I had made it without getting pregnant. I quickly busted her bubble and told her not to celebrate until I was 17 just to make sure that she didn't jinx it. Melody had given birth to me when she was 16 years old. When she turned 18, she changed her name from Melanie to Melody to harmonize with Symphony. Then she had Harmony four years ago and the rest was history.

I stop and am frozen stiff trying to figure out what that noise was I just heard. I look over at Harmony and she's curled up on the sofa still watching cartoons about to fall asleep any minute. I check the screen door to make sure it's still locked and go sit down next to Harmony on the sofa. I dial Melody again, still voicemail. *Ooh! She makes me so sick!* I contemplate if I should call Roman and see if he wanted to stop by.

5 CHAPTER FIVE
HUNTER SANTOS

I have nobody. I have surrounded myself with people who are fake just because I need to talk to somebody.
~Nikki Reed

"Hola mameee." I laugh every time Quincy tries to speak Spanish.

"No suena bien tratando de hablar español."

"Huh?"

"Hey Quincy… Your Spanish is horrible." I look over and see Roman. "Heey, Ro."

"What's up with that?"

"What's up with what, Quincy?"

"You open the door with attitude and just say, hey Quincy your Spanish is horrible, but you had to sing Ro's greeting! Heeeey Roooo!"

I start laughing. It felt weird seeing everybody after so long. I mean we Skype every now and then, but when I left, in my mind I had no intentions of coming back. This whole place is a joke. My so-called friends… are the biggest joke of them all. Look at Quincy now, all up in my face skinning and grinning. "Quincy, ain't nobody even say it like that." I took the scrunchie I wore on my arm like a bracelet and put my hair up in a quick bun. "Where you guys coming from?"

"Nowhere, really. Was just at the park chillin' with Symphony. You know she mad at you for not showing up to her little practice thing again." Roman said.

I shake my head as I close the screen door and stand on the stoop. "Ain't nobody thinking about her, she be out there dang near every day, practicing. That's just extra stuff. I told her I was thinking about quitting anyway." I just got back and already Symphony's trying to control somebody like she owns them. I have more important things to do besides jumping up and down and trying to cheer somebody on. It was cool in the past years because I wanted to be on the sideline cheering Q on… but not now.

"She ain't goin' like to hear that."

I shrug my shoulders to Roman's comment as Quincy stands close to me. "Forget all that. Won't you come through Symph's house?"

"Why?"

"I don't know. So we can chill."

"Hunter!" My mother yells from inside the house.

"What!" She doesn't answer back. "Mami, what!" Still no answer so I don't worry about it. I answer Quincy's question instead. "It depends on if I can get out or not."

"You've been gone for a whole year, Hunter. Since you been back, we still ain't have no chill time." Quincy whispered in my ear so that Roman couldn't hear.

"I know. I've just been so busy, moving back home, that's all. But you know I've been thinking about you the whole time." I pick through a couple of Quincy's dreads and wonder who he was chilling with the whole time I was gone.

"You betta. You bet not have been with no otha' nigga." And if I was? I look over at Roman whose too busy texting than to think about what we're saying.

"Please, that was the last thing on my mind." Quincy pulls me in for a kiss and I let him without hesitation. I don't know why. It just seemed like the normal thing to do. When people say Jaylen, you automatically think of Spirit. When people say Roman, you automatically think of Symphony. And when people say Quincy, you're going to automatically think of me. That's just the way it was.

"I'm about to leave you two lovebirds and swing by the crib right quick."

"Adios!" I said with the quickness. *Wasn't nobody thinking about Roman.* He was probably sitting there texting Symphony the whole time. So, who cares? Go be with her. Quincy and I stand on the stoop making out with each other until one of my twin brother's come to the door.

"Eww! I'm tellin'!"

Next thing I know, my mother is calling me to come in the house, saying it was time for Quincy to go home. Ugh! He just got here. I kissed Quincy goodbye one last time and go back into the house with much attitude.

"Hunter! My mother hollers again. "Get started on those dishes!"

I hated doing the dishes. Not that I was lazy but after dinner is a mess. People walk around all day snacking and drinking. Each time, my brothers are grabbing a different cup. After dinner, no one wants to empty their plates! "Mami! Why can't the twins help me?" I look at the mounds of dirty dishes invading the sink and I want to disappear. The dinner table is still plagued with dishes with scraps of food because no one wants to empty them into the garbage.

My mother is yelling at the boys to come and help me with the kitchen but of course, they're not moving. They're too busy thinking about their full bellies and video games. I wash about four plates when I notice that neither one of them has come to help and my mother forgot about making them.

I turn the water off and stump to their room, "Get up!" I yell at them as if I were they're mother.

"Hold on!"

"No! Come on and help me with the kitchen." I wait a few seconds. "Now! If I can't have fun then you can't either!" I tell both of them.

"Dead all that… we'll be there when we get done with our game."

"Mami, tell them to come on!"

My mother comes into the room with Josiah wrapped in a towel. "Go help your sister."

"Okay!" They're mouths agreed but they didn't bulge one inch.

I reach over and mess with Josiah's piggies. "Did you have a good bath?"

"Hunter, he's three months old, he doesn't know what you're talking about." My mother leaves out of the room and my brothers are still playing the game. I walk over closer to the electrical plug and fake as if I tripped pulling the plug from the socket. The TV and the whole game system goes black. For a moment, I think they were in complete shock because it was dead silence. All of a sudden, the twins lunge at me. I take off running towards the kitchen.

"I'm going to kill you!" They both shout in unison.

"Now you know how I feel… tattletale that!"

♥♥♥

As the twins were finishing the last of the dishes, I was wiping the kitchen table off when my cell began to vibrate in my pocket. I look at my cell and didn't recognize the number. Normally when that happens, I just press ignore and keep it moving. But this time, against my better judgment, I answer.

"Hello?"

"So it's true."

"Who is this?" I take the phone away from my ear and study the number again. Nope, no recollection.

"It's been a minute, so I'ma let you get a pass on that one."

As soon as I hear the laugh, I know exactly who it was. My cell slips through my fingers and I catch it just in time before it crashes to its death. "No!" I scream out as I look at the call slowly fading away as my fingers slide off the end button. Ohmigosh he's going to think I hung up on him! It's not as if I wanted to talk to him because I didn't. He's just not the kind of guy you hang up on.

I hand the dishcloth to my youngest brother, Jordan, and tell him to finish with the table. "Hecks naw! You better not leave!" Joey yells as he places a dish into the dish rack.

"Right! You said help you, we not doing it for you!"

"Justin, shut up! Just give me a second!"

I go into my room and close the door. Pacing back and forth, I contemplate on calling him back. I consider the consequences and repercussion of doing both. In my head quickly, I'm thinking, if I call him back, he might believe that I didn't hang up on him. But then I'd have to have a conversation with him and he'll probably ask me all these annoying questions—"

My cell rings before I had a chance to fully figure out what I should do. I hesitantly press the send button and answer.

"Did we get disconnected? Or did you hang up on a nigga?"

"N-No…"

"No what? Because see I'm having a hard time believing that ma' girl would hang up on me? You still ma' girl right?" He laughs his laugh again and I'm feeling really intimidated at the moment.

I try to take a deep breath all the while I'm praying this conversation will end abruptly. "Y-Yea, I'm still ya girl." I try to laugh a little myself and play it off as if I'm not the least bit scared of him. "My fingers accidently hung the phone up… my bad. You know I wouldn't intentionally hang up on you!"

"I'd like to think not. You've been home for a minute now. How come you ain't got at me?"

"Huh?"

"Hunt, sweetie, I'm a busy man. I ain't got time to play games like you ain't hear a nigga, now c'mon, babes."

"I didn't have your number."

"Well, you have it now. Lock that shit in and don't be afraid to use it. Matt-o-fact, you better use it." He laughs again. It's never a laugh like something is funny. More of a taunting laugh. "Anyways, Hunt?"

"Yes?"

"You got anything you want to tell me, babes?"

"Huh?" I correct myself before he does it for me. "I mean, like what?" I can feel the sweat pouring from my armpits.

"You tell me sweetie. I'm sure you know better than I do."

I had no idea what he was talking about. "What? That I missed you?" I really didn't I was glad he was out of my life. I hated to be talking to him now.

"I dunno, did you?"

"Yes." I lied. "Did you miss me?" I hated myself for even letting that flow from my lips.

"I can show you betta' than I can tell you. We'll hook up soon, but lata for all that… right now I got some business that I need you to handle for me. Think you can do that?"

"Patrón, you know all you gotta do is ask."

"That's my *nena*."

6 CHAPTER SIX
ROMAN DAVIS

Solitude

Loneliness expresses the pain of being alone and solitude expresses the glory of being alone.

~Paul Tillich

THIS IS THE BEST time of the day. Not necessarily because its night, but because I'm alone in my room. Just my beats and me. Usually my grandmother's in one ear and Symphony's in the other, both yappin' about something. If it ain't that, then I got a room full of niggas trying to play Madden or want me to make them a beat. Half of them can't rap and the other half wants something for free.

I like to be in solitude when I create. My mind clear and free from any outside drama. That's another reason why I'm glad Hunter is back. Now maybe Q will get off of mine. I have goals, not dreams. Just like in that old movie, 'Don't Be a Menace to South Central While Drinkin' Yo Juice in the Hood' "Dreams are fo suckas!" I'm already peeping out the latest colleges for either the best Music Arts program or Business.

I plan to be one of the best music producers one day. I figure I already have the talent in music, but who knows… you can never stop learning. With the football skills I have, I hope to get a free ride by getting a football scholarship.

If Symph and I get married one day, we should be set. Me and my music biz and her with her clothing line, we will be rollin' in dollars.

Q taps me on my shoulder knocking me from my solitude. "Take that plug out so I can hear too… is that my shit you working on?"

See what I mean? I can't catch a break. "Sup man, thought you would be chillin' at Hunter's house for a minute."

"Thought so too, but her mom's went back into trip mode."

"That sucks…"

"I wish! Thought I was goin' get—"

"You need to clean up this room!" My grandmother chimes in cutting Q off from his dirty mind. "Pick up them CD's and clothes off the floor boy."

"I am Ma!" My cell rings and the caller ID says it's Symphony. "What up bae?"

"Where you at?"

"The crib."

"Oh."

I pull the plug from my headset, my beat intertwines with Q's lyrics pouring into the airwave, and it sounds sick! Dun Dun… Dun Dun.

"Ohhhh!" Quincy places his fist to his lips and looks amazed as if he didn't think our collab would be fiyah. Dun Dun… Dun Dun. He nods his head along with the beat in deep thought. "Yeah… Hell yeah!"

"Nigga… as if you ain't know. Just needs a little tweaking here and there, but yeah."

Quincy continues to rap along with the beat, checking his hooks, and making sure that everything is flowing as it should be.

Every day I wake up, Son of a Battlefield
So hard to look up, Son of a Battlefield
Just wanna give up, Son of a Battlefield
'Cause I can't take it, I just can't take it

And all of a sudden. It all becomes official. My beat and his lyrics met and said, 'I do'. If ever there were such a thing as marriage between a beat and a lyric… this was the ceremony right here.

Q and I were so into this moment that I had forgot all about Symphony on the other end of the phone. I mentally prepare to be cussed out because I know she was going to let me have it. "Sorry 'bout that bae."

"Not a problem. I enjoyed listening."

"You must be home by yourself again."

She sighs and says, "Of course… Harmony's here though."

"You want me and Q to swing through?"

"That'd be nice. I'll order a pizza and see if Hunter wants to come by too."

"Aight cool. Let me finish up here and we'll be on our way."

♥♥♥

"Aye, lil homie, let me holla at y'all for a minute." Patrón and Remy sat in front of their parking lot in Remy's silver Cadillac.

"Here these niggas go." Q was already happy to make his way over to them.

"First question… how y'all lil scroungie niggas got two of the baddest chicks in the complexes?" Patrón asks from the passenger side window.

"Ha ha… well you know…" Quincy gives Patrón dap from the window.

"Y'all playin' in Saturday's game, right?" They both get out of the car and lean on the hood.

"No doubt!" Q answers for me.

"Y'all wanna make some bread?" Patrón finally spoke while puffing on a blunt.

"Hell yeah… what we gotta do?" Q steps closer but I stay planted where I am. Everything about these dudes spells trouble all the time. Nothing good ever came from dealing with Remy and Patrón.

"Aight… aight…" Remy puts his arm on Q's shoulder as if what he's about to say is top secret. "It's simple… I just need y'all to throw the game when y'all get up against the Cougars."

"Huh... that's it?"

"That's it."

"What?" I know he didn't just say what I thought he said. I'm MVP on my team and I ain't trying to throw nothing but a football!

"If ya punk ass wasn't all the way over there then maybe ya would have heard what I said." Remy turns and looks at me. Trying to intimidate me and put fear into my heart. They operate that way.

"Man, throwin' a game is like throwing away any chances of being seen by a recruiter or getting a scholarship. Plus we undefeated… I ain't 'bout to do that."

"This lil nigga think he hard, P."

"I see that."

"Nigga, you a Sophman, barely a sophomore. I could see if you was like, P, here." Remy smacks his brother lightly in the chest. "He a junior… ain't no recruiters lookin' at y'all young ass right now noway."

"Yo, let me talk to my man and we'll get back to y'all… I'm in either way 'cause I could use the bread." Quincy looks at me as if telling me to get on board.

♥♥♥

"Well, I don't see what the big deal is, just throw the game." Hunter takes her shoes off and slides her bare feet under her as she sat on Symphony's living room sofa.

"You don't see what the big deal is because you have no idea where

Roman is." Symphony sits the pizza box on the coffee table and grabs the paper plates. "You want some of this?" Symphony offers Hunter a slice.

"No, I'm good, I already ate."

"Anyway, Roman was Westbrook's first freshmen all state with the most total yards from scrimmage."

"Two-thousand plus yards… but go ahead and school 'em bae." I pat Symphony on her back as I reach and grab a slice for myself.

"And he was named first string offensive player and defensive player for city and state."

"So, who cares about all that? I'm talkin' bout fast money, cash, right now in our hands!" Quincy stands up to emphasize his point. "Just like Remy'em said… ain't no recruiters checkin' for you right now!"

"Man you sound crazy! Freshmen year I already had recruiters checkin' for me!" I get up too and pound my hand with my fist to prove my point.

"Alright, alright, alright!" Symphony stands in the middle of Quincy and me. "I ain't invite y'all over here for all this. Now ain't nobody throwing no game… PERIOD!"

"Y'all all know that Remy and Patrón don't throw out no play money. The less we probably get is $500 a piece!" Quincy calms down and tries to explain his point of view. "I don't know about y'all but a brother like me can use it!"

Symphony slaps Quincy's ball cap off his head. "I know you ain't stupid enough to get it in with them weed heads!"

"Man, Ro… you betta get ya girl!"

"I don't know. I'm with Q on this one." Hunter turn towards me and looks me in the face. "Please Ro, you do not want to get them dudes on your bad side. Take it from me and just do whatever they ask and leave it at that."

"What?" How does she sound telling me to do something like that? "I'm sorry, maybe I've never had the chance to introduce myself." I walk over to her and grab her hand to shake. "I'm Roman Davis. MVP of Westbrook Tigers Football Team." Even Quincy had to laugh on that one.

7 CHAPTER SEVEN
SYMPHONY PERKINS

Designers want me to dress like Spring, in billowing things. I don't feel like Spring. I feel like a warm red Autumn.
~Marilyn Monroe

"DO YOU THINK IT was wise to send those two together to get some bottled water?" Hunter ask me as I search through the dresses I designed.

"Uh, yeah! I'm not drinking no faucet water."

"Girl, I'm saying because the two of them were so heated when they left."

"They are not about to be fighting over that mess. Besides, dudes don't really fight over stuff like that. Girls, maybe. Well… not me…" I look at my hot like fire nails and blow on them as if they were just painted. "I'm not trying to break a nail fighting no *THOT*."

"If you say so… let you find out Roman got a side chick, I bet you break all them nails off yourself."

"And you ain't never lied! But I guarantee that wouldn't be the only thing I'd be breaking." I find the dress and hold it up to me in order to show Hunter. She doesn't see because she's too busy texting. I walk over to see who was more important than my designs and she holds the phone to her chest.

"Dang!"

"Let me see." I try to snatch the phone from her but she holds onto it even tighter and throws herself onto my bed so I couldn't get to it. "Is it that serious?"

"Obviously!"

"Well fine… if you want to keep secrets, I'm not giving you this dress."

"Geesh, Symph… do you want to see my man's thang-thang that bad?"

"Ew! He texted you a pic? While he was walking to the store?" Hunter gives me a blank sarcastic stare. I hand her the dress and tell her to try it on.

"I like this!"

"I know right!" She starts to head out of my room and I stop her. "Where you going?"

"To the bathroom to try it on."

"So try it on… why you have to go to the bathroom? It ain't like we ain't never changed in front of each other before… unless you have some wholly molly granny panties on." I crack up laughing.

"Nah, I just have to use it so I figure I'd just change while I'm in there."

"Why you gotta take your phone too? I know you're not thinking about texting him any pics back from my bathroom? She laughs, turns around, and looks at me with a mad face. I wave her off and say, "Hurry up I want to see it!"

Hunter goes to the bathroom to change and comes back and the dress looked better than I had imagined it. "Girl, yes! That is definitely you!"

"I know right! Girl, you outdone yourself on this one!"

"That shade is perfect with your skin tone!" I grab by cell and start snapping photos.

"Unh unh… my hair is not done for all that!"

"Please, Hunter… I am not interested in your face! I am getting the dress and the dress only." I like to take pics of my creations and place them in my design book. In it, I have the beginning sketch along with a sample piece of the fabric and a pic to complete each design. "I'm going to have to start charging you." I tell Hunter as she returns to the bathroom to change out of the dress.

♥♥♥

After I come from grabbing me a chocolate milk, I see an extra tray sitting at our table in front of a pink and purple backpack. "Whose is this?" I ask curiously.

"I think that's what's-her-face." Quincy began to snap his finger as if it were a mechanism for jump-starting his memory. "Damn, what the hell is her name? You know, the one girl that was at the park the one day."

"I know it ain't the freshman, Amber." I say looking at the stupid backpack in the chair.

"Yea... Her. Thought you ain't know her name." Quincy teased.

"Why the hell is her stuff at our table?"

Q shrugged his shoulders and continued eating as if he really didn't care. "I dunno. Think Ro or Hunter told her to come over here."

"Why the hell would they do that?"

Quincy pushed his tray away from him and looked at me as if I was irritating him. “I said, I don't freakin' know! Now should I stop eating just so I can accommodate you in a freakin' game of 20 questions?"

Sometimes.... No, scratch that! At all times! I can't stand Quincy's dumb ass! "I don't know whose bed you climbed out of the wrong side on but you might need to go back and try it again. Don't take it out on me because you’re unsatisfied!"

"I climbed out of yours!"

"Nigga you wish!"

The one thing I hated about Roman was that he always had to play the Good Samaritan. Well, I guess that's where he and I were different. The more I stared at her tray, the more it pissed me off. I know this chick ain’t trying to get in where she wished she fit in. I slam my bag on the middle of the table, sit my food and myself down, and slide my bag across the table, sending Amber’s food crashing to the floor. "Oops!” I said looking at her fries, burger, and salad co-mingling together on the floor.

"Now that was just dumb, stupid, and selfish!” Q said as he eyeballed the mess on the floor. "I know you did that shit on purpose too!"

Great! Usually no matter how much Quincy got on my nerves, he always appreciated one of my good jokes or devious plans. I guess Roman must be rubbing off on him. "Don't tell me you getting soft on me Q."

"He'll naw! I'm just saying, you could have given a nigga a heads up... I could have grabbed those damn fries!"

As we sat there laughing at the mess on the floor, I see Roman and Amber walking towards us with food trays in their hands and Hunter walking towards us empty handed coming from the restroom. At this moment, I'm puzzled like a mug. "Q? Are you sure that was Amber's tray?"

"It was sitting right there in front of her bag!" He assured me.

That nigga bet not have played me!

"What the heck!" Hunter yells referring to what appears to be her food on the floor.

At this point, I was speechless. Technically, I would just tell my girl the truth right here and now and possibly just buy her another lunch. But hell, I can't look like an ass in front of that nobody ass chick. And I damn sure can’t afford no more points adding up on Roman's bad side. But then again, forget 'em both because somebody invited that *thot* over here. So regardless whose food it was... It's gone now! "I didn't know it was your food?" I said to Hunter who was looking at me as if she wanted to kill me. *Damn, was the bitch that hungry? She can swerve with all that!*

"Would that have made any difference? Knowing whose food it was?" Roman the rescuer spoke.

"What do you mean; would it have made a difference? I wasn't the one who put it down there!" I lied trying to save my own ass. "So yeah it may have made a difference because if I had known it was Hunter's I would have got her another lunch."

"But why would you have done that if you didn't do anything to it in the first place?"

"Roman... You ain't the only nigga that can have compassion! You act like I don't have a decent bone in my body!" Sometimes I hate his self-righteous ass!

I began to plead the fifth and then Quincy spoke. "Dang bruh! It was an accident, okay? I dropped the shit down there, so what!"

"So what!? That was my food Quincy! Now what am I supposed to eat?"

"Mr. Q!" Mr. Morrison yelled from the other side of the cafeteria. "I'm a little jealous. Seems we had a lunch date and you stood me up! So you can spend the rest of the lunch period in my room now and for the rest of the week!"

Everyone in the cafeteria looked at Quincy and "Oh'd!"

"What you in for?" Roman asked.

"Man he caught me flickin' his class the other day. This some bullshit!"

"Well, least he didn't suspend you."

"Better for me if he did." He looked at Amber. "Hey Newbie... Pick that up for me." Without even thinking about it, Amber started to pick the food up from the floor.

"You ain't gotta do that." Roman said as he moved Amber out of the way and started cleaning it himself.

My stomach began to turn and suddenly I didn't have an appetite for my untouched food anymore. I slide my tray towards Hunter, "Bon appetite," and get up to leave.

It pisses me off how I have always been there for Roman at his every beck and call and he gone play me like that! As far as I'm concerned, he can do whatever the hell he want to and with whoever he want to do it with! I knew it was something I didn't like about that girl. She always be staring at Roman or me. For a minute, I was thinking that maybe she was a lesbian but when I see how she has to act all shy around Roman. Thotianna please! I am far from stupid or naive and his dumb ass is just falling into the trap. As far as pimple faced chick is concerned, she just made my shit list!

♥♥♥

SEPTEMBER

8 CHAPTER EIGHT

Throughout life people will make you mad, disrespect you and treat you bad. Let God deal with the things they do, cause hate in your heart will consume you too.
~Will Smith

THIS STUPID DAY IS *finally over. Took long enough!* Symphony was glad to head down the hall to her locker for the last time today.

"Sym-phony!" Roman yells her name from a distance.

She acts as if she didn't hear him and kept walking towards her locker. She'd be damned if she was about to carry any books home today. Symphony refused to walk around with a backpack like most of the lames looking like grade-schoolers.

The amount of homework these dumb teachers gave her were entirely too much. It had to be against the law. What are they doing in these teachers' meetings? They need to be discussing who giving out homework on what day and how much. Then again, maybe they do. *I betchu' they all have it in for me,* Symphony thought.

She neatly aligned all of her books in her locker according to her classes so that way she can just go and grab them within the little five minutes they give them to get to the next class. She slams her locker shut and roll the combination a few times. Don't ask why, it's just a habit she had.

"Oh, so you ain't hear me call you huh?" Roman was standing there waiting.

Not giving a damn, she didn't lie but kept it short. "I heard you."

"So why the heck didn't you stop, turn around, or acknowledge your ears were working then?"

"What, Roman?" She was still agitated and it showed but knowing

Roman, he didn't care. He had the nerve to invite that chick over to her table again. He knew that was her table and has been since they first started Westbrook. But the worst part about it is he knew how she felt but acted as if he didn't care.

"What is your problem? I know you ain't that mad about the girl?"

"Naw! I ain't mad about the girl, Roman!" Symphony said sarcastically. "You know I don't like her and yet and still you seem to keep inviting her to my table."

"So, you getting all out yo hook-up for what? It doesn't bother you to see someone constantly sitting by themselves? You of all people should know what it feels like to be alone, Symphony."

Symphony cocks her head and looks at Roman sideways. She felt like he was hitting her below the belt and she had no idea why. "You know what—" Symphony stops herself in mid-sentence and lets it go.

"So, what up wit' you? What you trying to get into?" He flashes his pearly whites at her. "Want to hang out?"

"I don't know. I got a lot of homework." She knew what kind of hanging out Roman wanted to do. She really want to tell him to go find that Amber chick and find out what she was doing. But she fought against it, jealousy never really looked good on anybody.

"Naw, really?" Roman responded sarcastically. "We pretty much got the same classes, so we might as well do it together." He places a strong emphasis on the two words 'do it' "Besides, I know you ain't about to carry no books home, so you might as well use mine."

He said exactly what she wanted him to say. Roman was far from being stupid or lazy. He knew how to get down with the books and always put his schooling first. Symphony knew that he'd be making it easier for her and she wouldn't have to use up all her brain cells to get all that homework done. Besides, why think if someone was going to do it for you.

Symphony loved looking at Roman and admired his sense of taste, but she wouldn't let him know all that. If you want a man, you gotta play hard to get. *But sometimes, it was hard trying to play hard,* Symphony thought to herself. Roman had that good hair that was naturally curly but he kept it shaved close to his head. You could tell he had nice hair by the way it lay down so smooth and thick and his waves can make a person seasick. He always dressed in the latest fashions and kept his kicks fresh and free from any dirt or creases.

The only thing Symphony thought was lame about Roman was that he carried an all-black backpack. At least it was Nike and not one of those $5 or $9.99 Wal-Mart Roll Backs. Plus, he wore his hanging off one shoulder, so she thought that was kind of cool.

"Here, put my folder in your bag." Symphony figured, why not be totally hands free. She took out her Win-Win pink lipstick from her bag and refresh her lips. Just as she was applying a thin layer of lips shine, she was interrupted.

"Hi, Symphony." An all too eager freshman runs up to her. She couldn't help but shake her head. "It's me, Amber? We sat together at lunch."

"Please don't remind me." She whispers to herself. "What the hell is up with your hair? "You need to seriously kill that backpack, fo-real tho." The freshman looks as though Symphony hurt her feelings. Symphony didn't give a damn, it wasn't like nobody give a damn about her feelings.

"Symp!" Roman calls out to get her attention and gave her a look that said, leave the little girl alone.

"What!" Symphony looks in Roman's direction. "You don't roll up in Westbrook speaking to me with no pink and purple backpack and to make matters worse, it's on her back! … and it's a Roll Back!" Symphony expresses to Roman as if Amber wasn't standing right there.

"Take it easy Symp." Roman said getting his laugh on. "She's just a freshman and having a little hard time fitting in." He touched Amber's shoulder and said, "You have to excuse her, she has "back-pack-aphobia"… a fear of backpacks." Roman sees his cousin Jaylen and run to catch up with him leaving Amber and Symphony standing there.

"Can I ask you a question?" The freshman continues without Symphony's permission. "Why do you hate me when you don't even know me?"

"Listen here little girl, you don't fool me. I peeped your game before you even thought about playing it."

"Huh?"

"See… why'd you even step to me and think you could even hold a conversation with me? Everybody up in here…" Symphony twirls her index finger in circles. "… want Roman. I see how them twins be disrespecting you… and you don't do nothing about it… because your weak."

Symphony looks at Amber and rolls her eyes. This little chick didn't have a clue who Symphony was or what she was capable of but Symphony had a feeling she was definitely going to try her.

♥♥♥

All Hunter wanted to do when she got home was to sleep. In American Government, Mr. Morrison, was so boring that she couldn't help but to catch some Z's in his class. Hunter thought she was safe sitting in the back. She propped her head in her left hand and kept her pen in the other hand on her notebook as if she were taking notes. Suddenly her eyes closed. It had to be a few minutes before her head dropped full speed heading for her desk. Thank God, she caught it before her face and desk were rudely introduced.

Hunter looked around the room embarrassed and hoping that no one had witnessed what just happened. No one had seen her except Quincy. He was over there shaking his head. Hunter knew he wanted to fall asleep just as she had with Mr. Morrison's monotone speaking self. She looked down at her notebook and discovered she hadn't taken any notes at all, just a bunch of scribble scrabble from her trying to fake as if she was awake.

As always, Symphony saves Hunter a window seat in the back with her. Hunter was still rather heated at Symphony for that stunt she pulled at lunch. Hunter thought, it just wasn't like Symphony to be so thirsty and over a freshman at that. She lay her head up against the window and close her eyes to rest while everyone else continued to board the bus.

"Aw Man! Hunter watch out!" Quincy's voice screams in Hunter's direction jerking her awake.

"What!?" She yells back startled.

"O, nothing. I thought your head was going full speed toward that window."

Hunter glares at Quincy. "Shut up!" Even more agitated than before, she regains her position alongside the window and closes her eyes again and listen as Quincy retells the events of what had taken place in Mr. Morrison's class.

Hunter didn't care and she wasn't the slightest bit embarrassed. She was too sleepy for all the nonsense. Quincy could be so immature sometimes. If he wasn't so annoying and always had to one up on Roman, he might have been a great catch to Hunter. She was too young to know if Quincy was Mr. Right… but she knew he was Mr. Right Now. He had a dark-skinned complexion and had grown his hair out for the past six months so he could get dreads. Hunter didn't mind the way Quincy's hair looked right now, she just didn't like if they got longer and turned into the big Rastafarian dreads. She like them on most people, she just didn't think they were the right look for Quincy.

Spirit and Jaylen, Roman's cousin, has been together since forever. For a young couple, they were doing the dang thang. Let Spirit tell it, they haven't even done the do yet. Symphony and Hunter try to tell Spirit, "If you ain't doing it with J, we guarantee you, he doin' some other chick you don't know about." But Spirit swears up and down that he's faithful and committed to their relationship.

Spirit and Jaylen both come and plop down in an empty seat in front of Symphony and Hunter. "Did you see her?" Sprit turns around and whispers to them.

"Who?" Symphony answers back.

"The girl I was telling Hunter about. The one I said I think she's crushing on Roman."

"Please don't even get that girl started." Hunter mumbles out loud referring to Symphony.

"O, you talking 'bout that freshman." Just then, Amber boards the bus with her two friends. "There she go right there." Symphony nudges Hunter until she physically had to look.

"Okaaay?" Hunter questions wondering why looking at a freshman was more important than her shut-eye experience.

"Tell her to come sit back here with us."

"You tell her! You probably want to just kick it on the girl anyway." Hunter turns her body so she was face to face with Symphony. "Are you that pressed over a freshman?"

Spirit was on her knees facing Hunter and Symphony all up in their conversation. "Turn around and quit gossiping." Jaylen pulls Spirit by her shirt. She did as he said but kept her ears glued to the back of her.

"Pressed!?" Symphony repeats three more times, as if she couldn't believe Hunter had even thought about letting those words pass through her lips. "When the hell have you ever seen me or known me to be PRESSED about anything, or anybody?" She cocks her head to the side and wait for Hunter to answer. Hunter kept silent trying to diffuse an already heated situation. "Oh, okay. I'ma remember that!" Symphony hissed and looked at Hunter and squinted her eyes as if they were about to secrete venom.

Hunter knew that Symphony was not the kind of person she wanted to have on her bad side. It wasn't as if she was scared of her, Hunter was just not in the market for making any enemies. Besides, Symphony and her have been friends for too long and she knew too many of Hunter's secrets. She wouldn't want Symphony to start running her mouth so Hunter motions for Amber to come to the back. She was sure Symphony was going to have a field day with the girl but it was out of her hands.

♥♥♥

Roman knew he was the smoothest brother at Westbrook High. Every girl wanted to get with him and every guy wished they were him. Everyone knew Roman, or rather, what they thought they knew or what he wanted them to know. Even though he stayed mingling with the squad, they never knew what he was really feeling or what he was dealing with on the inside.

Yeah, everyone knew that his mother had left him with his grandmother without leaving a note, saying good-bye, or telling them where she was going. But what they didn't know was how bad the incident had hurt Roman. Sure, he made everyone believe he didn't give a damn and that it didn't bother him one bit, but deep down inside, it cut deeper than a machete slicing across his throat.

Symphony thought she was slick, always having to have her little minion crew… her flunkies that always did everything she said, Roman thought as he watched Symphony and her friends call Amber to the back. Roman knew that Symphony tried to control him, but he was way too slick for that. He wasn't about to have a chick running him. That's why Symphony was always salty; Roman wasn't one that could be controlled by the hands, thoughts, or words of another.

Sometimes, Roman just liked to piss Symphony off just because he could. He got amused seeing her come out of her hook-up because she always tried to be so cool as if she was untouchable. Like now, the only reason why she told Hunter to call Amber to the back was to mess with her, but Roman had another trick up his sleeves to mess with Symphony and get inside of her head.

As Amber approach the back, Roman stands up and say, "Sup. What's your name again?"

"Amber." Roman could tell she was shy and as inexperienced as they came. He peeped her out real quick. Virgin. Definitely a virgin. Had to be. She was too scared to even look him in the face. She was cute though, Roman thought. Would be even cuter if she had a shred of confidence. It was probably all those bumps on her face.

"Move Roman and let her by!" Symphony yells with extreme pisstivity in her voice. Symphony knew Roman as well as he knew her. That's why he ignored her and kept on with his plan. He move to the side and in an usher-like manner, offers Amber the window seat of where he was sitting.

"Oh! So that's the game you trying to play?" Symphony says as she sits with her girls becoming loud and obnoxious. "I see somebody want to get fucked up!"

Roman could tell that Amber was starting to become uncomfortable so he tried to make small talk to ease her nerves. "So what you think about Westbrook High?"

"I like it."

Damn that was it? He was waiting on her to say something more or try her best to make the answer a little longer than that. Roman licks his lips and readjust himself sitting a little closer to Amber. He could feel her shaking. He laughs a bit and touches her arm but she snatches away from him with the quickness. Now, Roman was sitting there baffled. No chick has ever not wanted him to touch her.

He continues with the conversation and let her know that it didn't faze him none. "What you like about it so far?"

"I dunno."

It was literally like pulling teeth to get her to talk to him. As he's trying to talk to Amber, Symphony gets louder and louder.

"I should go over there and snatch the rest of her hair off her bald ass head!"

Amber began to feel self-conscience by symphony's threat because she began to sink down into the seat and fidget with her hair. That's one of the things Roman hated about symphony, she always had to be this big tormenter for no reason at all.

"Calm down. You lookin' real thirsty right now. You must be ready to start breaking those nails off." Hunter says to Symphony.

"Nah, fuck that! You wouldn't be saying that shit if Q's ass was doin' that mess, now would you? You got a lot of nerves calling somebody thirsty! Was you thirsty last year when Q broke your heart so bad ya ass had to leave town for the rest of the school year?"

"Symp!" Roman looks over and yells at her. "You need to calm all that down! All that ain't even called for!"

"Nah, what you doing ain't even called for!" She yells back.

Amber starts to get up but Roman holds her arm for her to sit back down. "What is you doin?"

"I'm just going to sit back in the front. It's too much drama back here for me."

"I got yo drama thotianna!" Symphony yells overhearing Amber's comment. "Don't get to happy sittin' where the hell you sittin'. He only got you sitting there because he knows it will piss me off!" Symphony looks at Roman and winks her eye. "He loves the make-up sex which he won't be getting when we get off this bus!" Like I said, Roman knows how to push her buttons and she knows how to push his.

A car pulls up alongside the bus with bass bumping. Roman is grooving to the beat until he see whose driving. Amber see them too because she ducks down even further. It's Remy in the car with the twins sitting in the back. Remy sees Roman, taps his watchless wrist, and points his index and thumb at Roman as if pointing and shooting a gun. Roman looks back and sees Quincy shaking his head.

"I'm telling you… that right there, ain't no idle threat." Quincy leans forward and whispers to Roman.

"Man please, I don't know what he's doing that for… I didn't make a deal with the devil, you did."

9 CHAPTER NINE
AMBER STYLES

Life is a song - sing it. Life is a game - play it. Life is a challenge - meet it. Life is a dream - realize it. Life is a sacrifice - offer it. Life is love - enjoy it.
~Sai Baba

I STAYED ON THE bus so I could get off at Willow'em stop and walk back down like I normally do. I couldn't believe all that just happened. I pinched the sleeve of my shirt and used the material to scratch the eczema on my arm. Ugh! I wanted to scratch so bad after Roman had touched my arm right there it was driving me nuts!

"Oh my gosh y'all." I run to catch up to Willow and Ryder. "Aaaaahhh! Can y'all believe that?" I scream and laugh at the same time.

It was pure silence. I felt like I was talking to myself. "What's up? Like why y'all trippin'? I readjust my backpack.

Willow starts looking around like she was looking for something. "Ryder? Do you hear anything?"

N-N-N-ope. N-N-Not n-n-n-othing." Ryder had a stuttering problem but seemed to only get worse when he was telling a lie.

"O, come on y'all. This is like one of the happiest days of my life, and this how y'all goin' do me?"

"You know, its mighty funny how you just forgot about us?"

"No, what's mighty funny is how you ran and left me that time but we ain't goin' talk about that, are we?"

Willow folds her arms across her chest and taps her feet. "Amber, I already apologized about that so just let it go!"

I can't believe how my best friend is seriously hatin' on me right now.

"Fine. But Willow, y'all could have come back there and sat just like I did." I found myself having to explain my decision. I knew full well if anyone of them had invited Willow and Ryder to the back, any one of them would have flown in the back of the bus. But then again, maybe not because they like being a nobody.

"B-b-but we weren't invited, just you!" Ryder chimed in.

"I know right!" I couldn't help but sing it while I pop my collar and dust my shoulders off. I couldn't contain my happiness. All my school life, I had been waiting for a day like today, it has finally come, and I had no one to share it with. It really sucked that they were my friends and couldn't be happy for me.

'Ugh haters,' I mumble to myself.

"I wouldn't have gone back there anyways." Willow began. "Those who want to ride in the back of the bus are ignorant. Ignorant to the facts of how and why we fought so hard to be able to sit in the front."

Blah, Blah, Blah. I mean can she get any more boring. I mean she couldn't possibly be serious, like we don't know our history. I couldn't contain myself any longer. "Why is you hatin' Willow?" I stop walking, take my backpack off my back, and slide it to the ground.

Willow turns around and walk back to where I stop. "Ain't nobody hatin'." Willow rocks her neck back and forth. "I just don't think they're the kind of people you should be hanging with. I think they are just trying to set you up for failure."

"OMG Willow! You act like somebody is going to take my friendship away from you!" I get close up in Willows face and purse my lips.

Mimicking me, Willow said, "Honey please, that's the least of my worries. If someone could take your friendship from me, I gladly give it. Just like when you decided to go to the back! And when they turn around and hurt your feelings, don't come crying to me about it!"

"Oh, don't worry I won't! You'd probably run away anyhow!"

♥♥♥

I am glad to be rid of the two killjoys. I wasn't about to let nobody still my joy today, I was too happy. I use my house key to open the door because my mother's car wasn't in the driveway. I checked the refrigerator and my mother had a note pinned to it letting me know that she had some errands to run with my grandmother and would be back soon.

My mother has always been a stickler for rules. After school, me and Cam'Ron are to always come straight home, no matter what. We're to have no company what-so-ever, not even Willow or Ryder. Soon as we get in, we have to change our school clothes, do our homework, and straighten up the house. Those rules are to be followed rather or not she is home. Half the time Cam'Ron doesn't even follow them, but I do. I am not trying to get into any trouble.

One thing we didn't have was a curfew. That was because we were not allowed to be anywhere without my mother, grandmother, or father. If we are outside playing, we have to be in before the streetlights. Yes, my mother was that over-protective.

I go into my room, change out of my school clothes, and fall back onto my bed and daydream about Roman and me. I wonder, if Roman and Symphony were together all like that, why he asked me to sit with him. If Roman was with Symphony, there was no way that he would have did what he did in front of Symphony's face. Besides, he was the one who came to me and asked me to sit with him at lunch. Even though Symphony was acting funny, it sure beat sitting at a lunch table with random people I didn't know or by myself. I hated that Ryder and Willow didn't have the same lunch period as me, but I'm cool eating lunch with my bae.

Maybe I was just making a big deal out of nothing. I tend to do that from time to time. But not this time, I enjoyed the feeling I got when Roman sat next to me. I loved the way he smelled, his smile, his teeth, and the way his shimmery silver watch glistened against his bronze colored skin tone.

I search through my closet for something to wear to school tomorrow. I had to make sure that I was extra fly. My heart fell into my belly. What if he asks me to sit with him on the bus in the morning? I grin a devilish grin. Aww man, if that happened, Willow would be sooooo mad! O well, forget her… she'll get over it. I pick out the cutest newest outfit I had.

♥♥♥

Cam'Ron comes crashing through the door like the Tasmanian Devil and runs into the bathroom.

"What's wrong with you? I speak into the brown wooden door.

"Nothing."

"Something is." I try to turn the doorknob as if I didn't know he had already locked it. I lean up against the door and wait for him to come out. After waiting for about five minutes, Cam'Ron swings open the door, making me fall back and lose my balance. He grabs a frozen bag of peas from the freezer and places it over his left eye.

I try to see what he's hiding on his face by reaching up and trying to remove the peas.

"Mooove!" He shoves me.

"Cam'Ron let me see!"

"Why? So you can tell mommy?"

"From how you're making it seem, looks like ma will find out on her own."

Slowly he moves the bag of peas from his eye and I jump back and gasp.

"Is it that bad?" He throws the bag of peas onto the kitchen table and run back to the bathroom mirror. "Damn!"

I thought my cheek was messed up before but his eye is jacked! When my mother asked about my face, I just told her as I was about to come out of my room, Cam'Ron was busting in and the side of the door hit me in the face. Of course, Cam'Ron gladly took the backlash from that. Why? I don't know. She yelled at him a little and told him to stop hopping and jumping around so much.

"Were you fighting?" He looks at me as if I'm a moron.

"Nah!" He says sarcastically. "I slipped on my bed and hit my pillow!" Examining his eye closer in the mirror made him become even angrier. "I know I'm going to get in trouble for this!"

"Who were you fighting with this time?"

"I wasn't fighting…"

"You just said you were fighting."

"'Cause you pissed me off asking stupid questions!"

"Why are you getting mad at me? I didn't do it!"

Cam'Ron looks at me and sits on the edge of the tub. "I wasn't fighting… not this time anyway. I was standing by the bus talking to Justin after school and then TJ throws the football at me saying think fast… after he threw the ball and hit me in the face."

"A football did all that to your face?"

"Shut up and leave me alone!" Cam'Ron goes into his room and slams the door. I leave him alone because I know he's going to go through it as soon as my mom gets home.

♥♥♥

I finished my homework and chores, I even did Cam'Ron's cleaning for him because I felt so bad. Now I was left with nothing else to do. My mom should be coming in soon and I was bored and starting to get hungry. By now, Willow and I would be knee deep in conversation. I guessed that Willow was still mad since she hasn't called.

I pick up the phone to dial Willow's house. I guess I would have to be the bigger person. "Hello?' Willow answers on the third ring.

"What you doin'?"

"Nothing." Willow was being short with me so I deducted that she was still upset.

"Look. We've been friends for too long to be going through this."

"Going through what? I'm cool."

Yeah, okay. If she was cool, why is she talking so dry?

Silence.

I remove the hamburger meat from the refrigerator and brown it in a pan.

"What are you doing?" Willow finally asks breaking the silence.

"Girl, browning meat for Sloppy Joes." I couldn't wait on my mother any longer. I hoped my mother would be happy that I was taking the initiative. Besides, in my head, Roman and I were already married and he hadn't quite gotten home from work yet. Instead of Sloppy Joes, I was making fried chicken, greens, and mac & cheese, with a side of Jiffy Mix Cornbread.

"All right… I ain't going to lie." Willow says hesitantly. "I guess I was a tad bit jealous."

Ha! I knew it ya hater! I want to throw Willow's confession in her face since she was such a killjoy this afternoon but I decide to act mature and let the little situation go. I place myself in Willow's shoes and thought I'd probably had reacted the same way if not worse. Instead, I said, "Girl, ain't no reason to be getting jealous."

"Says you! I am not a hater though. However, I am happy for you Amber. You said you were going to be popular this year and find yourself a boyfriend, I guess you doing it. But keep in mind, stuff like that, always comes with some kind of price to pay."

What? Whatever! I wanted to ask her how much 'cause I'd gladly pay it! I had to admit to myself that I was finally doing it and my goals were finally being achieved. "See Willow, It's all in who you know. You gots to get in where you fit in." I was now teaching Willow and hoping she was taking notes.

"Is that right!" Willow laughed.

"Yeah, because see… I guess I should be thanking you for leaving me, if it wasn't for that, Roman probably wouldn't have even noticed me."

"But why would you want someone to notice you only when something bad happens? If he was really interested, he would have noticed you anyway."

Huh? What they heck is she saying? I sprinkle some sugar into the Sloppy Joes, place a lid on top, and turn the knob to simmer.

"Willow?"

"Huh?"

"Is you over there still sippin' on some Hateraid?" Finally, we both started laughing until my jaws were starting to hurt.

"Nah, but for real though, what did he say to you anyways."

10 CHAPTER TEN
HUNTER SANTOS
Loud Silence

"HUNTER! HUNTER!"

I lay there on my bed fully clothed with my shoes still on listening to my mother call me. I can never get any sleep! I punch my pillow with my fist and place the pillow over my head to try to drown out my mother.

"Hunter! I know you hear me calling you! Hunter!"

Even from under my pillow, I can still hear my mother calling and cursing me out in Spanish, thinking that the little ones wouldn't catch on. Frustrated and already knowing what my mother wanted, I yell out, "Mami, What?"

"Ay, Hunter! What is this? You lay there sleeping. I would like to be able to lay down to ya know! But No! I have to take Josiah to daycare, go to work, clean and cook, all while you take it easy sleeping! No way missy!" My mother, Marie, lay Josiah on top of my chest.

"Ugh! Mami, he stinks!

"Yup! Change him!" My mother takes the burp cloth off her shoulder and toss it onto the bed.

"Why didn't you change him before you brought him to me?"

She turned on her heels to face me. "Because Hunter –"

"Sup!" My brother comes crashing into my room interrupting.

"Jordan, go get me Josiah's diapers and his wipes."

"Okay, where they at?"

"I dunno! Ask Mami." Jordan leaves out of my room yelling at the top of his lungs for my mother to find the diapers and wipes.

I'm so cranky and irritated because I haven't been able to get any sleep lately. It was six of us all crammed like sardines inside a three bedroom ranch style house. There was no upstairs, no attic, no basement, not even a garage. There is no peace for me here. I can't wait until I turn 18 and get a place of my own. Don't get me wrong though, I love my family, but sometimes, it was just too much.

"Jordan, bring me the stuff!"

"I'm coming, hold the freak on!"

I change Josiah's diaper and reminisce about the days when I would be included in charging my father at the door. Usually I couldn't wait until Papi got home because he would always bring me something. I didn't care if it was a new pair of shoes, jump rope, or a 50-cent bag of chips. He'd done it as long as I could remember, but not now. Now, was a different story. So many things have changed.

My brother, Justin, one of the more mature twins comes into my room, grabs Josiah, and plays with him. "What's up between you and Papi?"

"Nothing. Why do you ask?" He sits on my floor and hands me a rubber band. I brush his long, thick, curly hair back and place it into a ponytail.

"It just seems like since you and mami came back from grandma… it's just been a lot of tension. I mean, it was a lot of tension while y'all was gone too. He and Mami argued a lot over the phone."

"I know, I heard it from my end too."

"You know what it was about?"

"Not really…" I can hear Jordan and Joey fighting over a video game.

"Pipe down all that noise in here!" My father roars as he walks in the door.

"Dad!" Jordan ran to my father to tattletale on everything that Joey had said or done.

My father, Terry, was tall dark-skinned man who towered over people like a giant. He spoke in a deep tone and had permanent wrinkles etched across the top of his forehead from too much worry and un-forgiveness.

My father sat on the edge of his bed removing his work boots. After releasing his toes into the air, he places his sock up to his nose and takes a whiff. Jerking back from the wretched smell, he balls his socks into each other and throws them into a corner.

I stand by the threshold of their bedroom door with Josiah planted on my hips. I was tired of the silence between us and him treating his firstborn like a stepchild. I swallow hard and clear my throat. "Papi, Hi." I say in a low tone focusing on the tattered corner of a throw rug that flowed from beneath my parents' bed. I wait for the sound of his voice to respond before I move or say another word.

"Close the door. I need to change my clothes.

11 CHAPTER ELEVEN
SYMPHONY PERKINS
Tick for Tack

I LAY ACROSS ROMAN'S bed with my math homework spread out in front of me. Two more problems and we are done for the night. We had been studying for over two hours. Well, not the whole two hours because sometimes we would be engrossed into conversation or may have stopped to play a game of Madden on Roman's new PlayStation.

Yes, underneath this frilly girly exterior, I knew how to and loved to hang with the fellas. I didn't dare wonder about the guys thinking of me as another guy because with this physique, flawless face, and skills, they all knew what time it was.

That's one of the things I knew Roman loved about me. He didn't have to become a coach and teach me about football or basketball, because I already knew. Plus, I knew how to look good doing it.

"What you get for the last one?" I ask Roman as I scroll my cell, browsing through Facebook.

"Unh unh… no! You want the last one, you do it."

"Excuse me?" Who the heck was he talking too like that?

"I've given you the answers to every problem and I don't think you've answered not one."

"So…"

"So… how are you going to learn if you don't even try? You've been sitting on Facebook since you got here. If you'd put as much effort in your homework as you do Facebook… I'm sure you'd have all A's and wouldn't be in jeopardy of getting kicked off the squad or losing your position as captain."

I know he did not just go there with me. "Oh I see, you want to throw out low blows huh?" I flick him off. "Whatever, I just can't stand Geometry."

"Well from now on, you are going to be doing your own math homework."

"I don't give a dayum. I don't need ya help no way."

"Where is Jaylen at?" Roman's grandmother sticks her head into his bedroom.

"I don't know Ma." That's what Roman started calling his grandmother after he found out that his birth mother wasn't coming back.

"Well, I need to speak to the both of you about something very important. But I'd rather do it when the two of you is here, alright?"

"Alright Ma." Roman says without looking up. He was too engrossed into his Madden and determined not to let me beat him this time. He had already finished his last math problem and left me hanging so to make him even more heated, I picked up a controller to whoop that butt.

"Boy! You betta turn 'round here and look at me! I'm talkin' to you." Roman reluctantly obliged his grandmother. "Now I'm 'bout to go to Bingo. Don't y'all be up in here makin' no babies, ya hear?" I crinkle my nose, look at his grandmother, and then at him. "How are you Orchestra?" And without waiting for me to respond, she left for bingo.

I hated when the old woman tried to be funny and make fun of my name. I had been coming over here for years and never, not once has the old bag got my name right. Whatever so-called witty name she would come up with, Roman never had my back. Instead, he would sit there laughing as if he was about to bust a gut.

"So, what's the deal with you and the freshman?" I can't lie, I was dying to know because I thought that stunt he pulled on the bus and at lunch was uncalled for. I didn't like to be made a fool of, and that's exactly what he did.

"Who Amber?"

"OH, we on a first name basis I see?"

"Why is you always trippin'? I'm on a first name basis with ALL your friends. You don't seem to be mad about that."

"First of all, she NOT my friend! I don't even know the girl!"

"Why is you gettin' all out yo hook-up?" Roman pauses the game and lay the controller on the floor.

I get up from Roman's bed and start stuffing my homework into my folder. I had to show him that I could get an attitude just as quick as he could. I want to ask him if he was really feeling that girl, but I didn't want to make it appear as if I was thirsty. "I'm about to go." I hold my folder in my hand ready and willing to leave the situation.

"Oh, that's how it is now. Just like that you're going to leave."

"Yes Roman, just like that." I could do a lot of things except back down or give in but only when it came to anyone else but Roman. It was hard for me to say no to him. Whenever he wanted sex, I gave it to him, no questions asked. But I know that if I wanted to keep him eating out of the palm of my hand, I was going to have to try to dish these goods out a little at a time. I had to be strong.

"Girl calm down. Ain't nobody into that lil' girl. I don't even know her either." Roman walk over and tried to soothe me. "You know I only mess with you."

"Then why the public display on the bus and at lunch Roman?"

"I just did that to piss you off." He smiles and tries to lean in for a kiss.

"Well guess what?" I push Roman away from me by mushing him in the face. "It worked!" I turn to leave out of Roman's bedroom door with the intentions of heading home. Roman catches me by the arm and pulls me back into his room. I look at his hand on my arm and he knows to let it go.

"My bad. Come on, we did all this homework, don't you think we deserve some chill time?" He bites into his lips and lick them. I look at him and roll my eyes.

"Roman, you ain't slick. I'm not some dumb female you can play with. I know what you're up to."

He tries to come in closer for a hug. "What am I up to?" Not waiting for an answer, he continued on. "I just figured we can order a pizza and watch this Redbox."

I don't know what type of fool he took me for, but I was going to play along until I got full off the pizza and then bounce. "Is it Pizza Hut?" I ask nonchalantly.

"Come on! You know I know you." Roman orders the pizza and pops this movie into his PlayStation to watch it. I didn't even know what the movie was called nor did I care. After I ate about three slices, Roman is all over me sweating. I knew my limits. I didn't let my mind go there. All the while, he was kissing and grinding on me, I kept seeing that girl Amber's face. No lesbo. I just couldn't concentrate but I guess that's a good thing because I didn't want to give him none no way. I push him off and tell him it's time for me to go.

"So, it's like that? Roman questions feeling offended.

"Like what?" I try to play stupid.

"You just goin' leave me like this?" I look down at the area of his sweatpants he was referring to.

"Nigga please! That's all you! Just like I have to do my Geometry myself… You have to do you, yourself." I roll my eyes at him. "Go take a cold shower!" He done pissed me off now! As if it was my fault, his soldier was standing at attention and my duty to put him at ease. Psst….

He can be gone with those shenanigans.

Roman strolls over and puts his arms around me to try and sweet talk me out of my underwear. "I don't know why you be trippin' girl. You know I love you."

"Uh huh."

"Oh, so you don't love me back?"

"Yeah I do, you already know that." I cross my arms across my chest."

"So what's up then?"

"I'm on my period."

"So why you ain't just say that then?" He jumps back and puts distance in between him and I.

"I'm on my period butthole! It's not a disease!"

"Ah, naw. I'm just messing with you." Roman comes back closer to me and whispers into my ear as if someone else was in the room. "It's other thangs you can do you know."

♥♥♥

It was something after 9pm when I had finally made it home from Romans'. I didn't even bother to come home first or even call to let my mother know where I was. My mother and I always gave each other our own space. We were cool like that. I could talk to my mother about almost anything. Some things were my business only just like my mother felt. Most of my friends thought I had the coolest mother; I felt the same way.

Melody was in her silk robe pouring two small glasses of Hennessy.

"Where's Harmony?" I say, asking about my little sister.

"Went to bed early. She was in her room watching SpongeBob until she fell asleep."

"Don't you want to ask me where I've been?" I question my mother.

"Honey, I know everything. You wasn't doing nothing but over that boy Roman's house."

"There's no surprising you is it?" I joke. My mother disappears into her room with the two drinks of Hennessey like she was about to get turnt up and I hear the door close.

I go upstairs to run me a nice hot bubble bath and decide I want to sneak a little shot of Hennessey for myself while I soak in the tub. I creep past my mother's bedroom and the floor made a loud creaking sound.

"Symphony! I left my cigarettes downstairs, can you grab 'em for me right quick?"

"Aight." Even better.

I snatch some toilet paper off the roll and head downstairs. Taking four Newport's out of my mother's pack, I wrap them in the toilet paper, and place another one in my mouth while I grab a plastic cup for my Hen.

Now don't sleep! My mother was cool but not crazy. She didn't allow me to smoke, turn up, or have sex but I managed to do it anyway without my mother's knowledge. Sometimes right under her nose.

On the real, I didn't like being downstairs by myself. It always felt eerie. That's why, whenever there was a light switch within my path, I would switch it on. Even with that being the case… it was okay coming but felt worse going. I turn the kitchen light off and run as fast as I can up the steps without making it too obvious I was running from something. What, I don't know. When I'm alone, it always feels like a presence is behind me. In the shadows lurking. But I don't tell nobody that though… and you better not either!

Melody's room was directly in front of the bathroom so the floor creaks again when I go inside the bathroom to lay my hide-aways down and turn the water off.

My mother cracks her bedroom door. "What's taking you so long?"

"I had to turn my water off."

"Uh huh." Melody has the door cracked only wide enough for me to barely get the Newport's through.

I turn Pandora on my cell phone to listen to some music as I chill out and soak but not too loud to where I'd wake Harmony. I sure didn't need her waking up and jumping in the bed with me because my mother's was occupied. Sometimes, if I had another one of those bad dreams where I couldn't move, I'd go in Harmony's room, pick her up and bring her to bed with me. I guess you could say she was like my real life teddy bear. I don't let nobody know that either. In the morning when she wanted to know how she got there, I'd tell her and my mother that she walked in there on her own. I 'bout have Harmony and my mother thinking the girl practically walks in her sleep.

I have no idea who my mother has in her room with her and why it's so top secret. By now, I would have met any dude my mother knew well enough to invite into her room at night. I knew my mother's business was her business but just like she always said to me, "I have to know all your friends and where they live just in case they find your body, I wants to be able to find them."

It made me wonder, what if something bad happened to my mother. I wouldn't even know where to start. I'm going to have to remember to have a serious talk with her. Then my mind drifts to Amber. It pisses me off that somehow lately she seems to invade my real life space and now it's as if she just barges her way into my mind. It's not like I'm having a guilty conscience experience because of how I treat her. I have good reason of treating her like that! That thot is up to something. I can feel it. I can tell she's real sneaky. I'ma have to watch her. O well, you know what they say… keep your friends close and your enemies closer.

The Newport is gone and so is the Hen. I'm sweating more than I'm getting clean. The Newport has definitely helped the Hen with my buzz and has me feeling right. Normally when I soak in the tub this late at night and everyone in the house is sleep, I leave the bathroom door opened or at least cracked. I couldn't tonight because my mother has some man in the house. And like I said, the bathroom is directly in front of her room.

I walk into my room and see my curtains blowing in the breeze. I try to remember opening my window. I walk over about to throw the ladder away from my window until someone covers my mouth from behind and tells me not to make a sound.

12 CHAPTER TWELVE
AMBER STYLES
Makeup Mishap

I WAS GLAD MY mother had gone into work early this morning, which had worked out fine for me. Cam'Ron is still sleep because he isn't going to school today. My mom made him a doctor's appointment for later on. When my mom came home, she flipped out when she saw his eye. He tells her what he told me but she didn't believe him. She called the school to ask about the incident and the principal did not collaborate Cam'Ron's story. He says Cam and another boy was in the boys' bathroom jumping another guy and Cam'Ron slipped and hit his face on the edge of the sink. He also tells my mom that he knows all this because someone had videoed the whole thing on their cell and showed it to him. So yeah, I'm sure he's going to be on lock down for a minute.

I told Willow to come over early so that I could fill her in on some more of me and Roman as I got dressed. Yeah, yeah… I knew I was breaking my mom's rule about not having company over after-school, but she never said anything about before school, so that would be my excuse in case I got caught. Besides, it was only Willow. We were practically family.

I sneak into my mom's make-up bag and begin to practice applying make-up. It takes me three tries until I was somewhat happy with it. I use black eyeliner to give myself the appearance of cat eyes. I used my mom's foundation, eye shadow, and red lipstick. I've seen a lot of movies of how people get a make-over and their life is changed in an instant. I need that instant life changing experience. I admire myself in the mirror and I have to say, I was looking fabulous. Another thing that made it so great is, I barely see my blackheads.

After my face was done, I give another attempt at my hair. I'm already dressed and there is still no sign of Willow. I grab my backpack to make sure that all of my stuff is inside. Then I hear Symphony's voice and Roman saying the she has back-pack-a-phobia or something like that. I search the house for something more suitable to use.

I look inside the back of my mom's closet and see a big black bag I don't remember seeing her use and thought that it would be perfect. It was practically empty beside a little bit of paper that was inside it. I empty it out and toss the papers onto my dresser.

♥♥♥

I hear a light tapping on the front door and swing it open to see Willow standing there. "What took you so long? It's almost time to go now!"

"It's dark as heck out here!" Willow strides pass me and into the living room. "It's even darker in here." Willow walks over and turns on the tableside lap. "OMG!" She starts laughing and snorting like a pig. "Why do you have all of that on your face? Seriously, go wash some of that off."

"What!? No!" I knew Willow was just being a hater as usual. I'm tired of her having the nice clothes, nice hair, and pretty straight white teeth. I can go on and on comparing myself to her. It was time for Willow to envy me for once.

"You know dang well, Ms. Joi would whoop your butt if she knew you was playing in her make-up."

"Excuse me?" I crinkle my nose and display my face with my hands as if it were a showcase item. "Does this look like playing to you?"

"Amber, I'm just saying it doesn't look right. You should take some tissue and try to blot it or blend it in or something."

"Hmm… what did you have for breakfast? Hatin' and eggs? And besides, when was the last time you wore make-up?" I put my hand to my ear. "Never, that's when. So you are the last person to give make-up tips.

After that, you know what Willow said? Nothing. Because she knew, I was right.

Me and Willow pretty much walk to the bus stop in silence until we get to the corner where we meet up with Ryder.

"Are we s-s-supposed to mee-meet up at the church today for practice or Sis-sis-ter Jackie's house?"

"At the church at 6:00pm." Willow replies.

"Y'all think Roman goin' ask me to sit with him this morning?" I say trying to break our long bout of silence.

"Ryder and Willow look at each other as if I was annoying them. The bus was about to pull up and the sun was finally starting to fill the sky with a dim light.

"W-w-what's wrong with your face."

"Ugh! Get on the bus stupid!" Now he and Willow both were about to annoy me.

My heart starts to beat faster and faster as each foot hits a step. I'm too scared to look up into the back and start to feel self-conscience of my make-up. I stand in the middle of the isle and wait for an invite from the back, but nobody said anything.

The bus doors close and I had to make a split decision to sit in my original seat but Ryder was already sitting with Willow.

"You're going to need to take a seat." The bus driver yells out making all eyes beam on me.

"Ryder, move out my seat." I demand, already feeling embarrassed.

"N-n-no, I thought you moved your s-seat. Go s-sit in the back."

"Oh, okay. I see how you are."

"Please take your seat. I can't pull off until you do."

I wanted to tell the bus driver to shut the hell up! I looked towards the back and everyone acted as if they were all sleepy. No one even said a word to me, except one idiot I didn't even know.

"Sit down, geesh!"

I rolled my eyes at him while looking for an extra seat. I found an open seat next to this person that no one ever wanted to sit by because he was so disgusting. He constantly picked his nose, farted, and looked like he never brushed his teeth.

Great! I thought to myself as I sat on the very edge of the seat. So far to the edge that if the driver hit a bump my rump would hit the floor.

When the bus had finally started to pull off, everyone had started clapping because I had finally sat down. Forget them! Acting like they can't wait to get to school.

Ryder turns around and looks at me. I stick my tongue out at him and cross my eyes. I was too scared to look behind me. I was sure they were all back there staring and talking about me anyway. Forget them too!

All through school, everyone was looking at me, snickering, and whispering. It wasn't like 'Hahaha and pointing fingers', but that's how it felt to me.

Since I wasn't invited to the back of the bus this morning, I decided to just sit by myself at lunch. I figured I was the out-cast anyway. What I felt I had gained yesterday all reverted to all those years back to elementary. I sat there sulking in my own misery and had no idea why things had changed.

♥♥♥

"Why you sitting here by yourself today?" Symphony sat down next to me.

I was sure Symphony just wanted to make-fun of me as well, so instead of verbally answering I just shrugged my shoulders.

"Have you been to the restroom at all today?"

What kind of freakin' question was that? I shook my head no and continued eating my fries.

Symphony picked up my tray of food and grabbed my arm. "Come on." Symphony told Hunter to watch my food while we head to the restroom.

When Symphony turned me toward the big glass mirror, I was horrified. "OMG!" I screamed. "What happened?"

"Let me guess. This is your first time wearing make-up, am I right?" I nodded and Symphony laughed. "And it's probably your mother's right?"

I nod again but this time tears run down my face and I wipe my wet eyes with the back of my hands smearing what used to be my eyeliner. How embarrassing! I have been walking around looking like a dang clown all day! And the most embarrassing part is Symphony had to be the one to point it out.

"Oh! No… no… no… See you just went from bad to worse. If you're going to wear make-up, there are a few rules." Symphony went rummaging inside her purse and pulled out another smaller looking purse that only appeared to have makeup supplies in it. "#1. Know your shades. #2. No cheap, roll back, discounted, or no name brand stuff. #3. Never, Ever Cry!" She pulled some face cream out of her purse. "Here rub this all over your face."

I did what she told me to do. At first, I didn't trust her but the way I see it, I couldn't look any worse.

"I take it your mom must be a few shades lighter than you?"

"Yeah, how'd you know?"

"Because the powder on your face looks like powder." Symphony laughed again. She appeared to be busting a gut at my expense but that was nothing new.

I wanted to take offense to her laughing at me but I guess she didn't mean anything by it. She was the only one helping me today.

I really didn't know how she was going to help me since she appeared to be lighter than my mom. She the one talking about, know your shade… I mimicked Symphony in my mind.

"This is actually Spirit's foundation. You two seem to be about the same shade." Dang! It was almost as if she read my mind. I was almost scared to think anything else at this point.

Symphony applied spirit's M.A.C. foundation on my face and redid my entire make-up. I had to admit, I looked so much better, I felt as if I was getting a real makeover. What I couldn't understand is why. Why would she do this for me? Maybe she was bipolar. Or maybe she does have a guilty conscience after all.

"What kind of make-up is that so I can get me some?" I rub my lips together to smooth out the reddish color lipstick she applied. Troublemaker. That's what she called it. I was about to get offended until she showed me the label. It really said troublemaker. She say that her Win-Win wouldn't look right on my skin tone but that it would go perfect with my backpack. I let her little pun go because she was doing me a solid. What I couldn't understand is, why not just say what it was… pink.

"Oh, no hun. You won't be able to afford this, I'm sure. I only use M.A.C. and it's expensive." Symphony started placing everything back into her purse. "You might be okay with Cover girl, Maybelline, or Elf."

"Oh, how much is that stuff?"

"A whole hell of a lot cheaper."

"But what about rule #2?"

"Hun, you have to crawl before you can run in the Olympics with the big girls." She placed the makeup bag back into her purse. "Hey, how's your math skills?"

"Okay, I guess."

"Okay? What does that mean? Do you get A's, B's, C's… what?"

"Oh… A's and B's I guess."

"You guess? What you've never gotten a report card?" She waves her hand and shakes her head at me. "Never mind… good enough. I got a way you can pay me back." She opens the bathroom door to leave.

"Well, thanks for helping me, Symphony."

"No worries. I wouldn't even want my worst enemy looking like you were." I think she rolled her eyes at me as she headed for the door.

13 CHAPTER THIRTEEN
SYMPHONY PERKINS
The Good Samaritan

I LEFT AMBER IN the restroom with the mirror while I went back to eat and kick it with my squad.

"Please tell me you didn't make that girl feel any worse than she already did, Symphony." Hunter dipped her fry into Quincy's left over ketchup.

"Now, why would I do that?" I answer a question with a question. "Y'all be acting like I'm a monster or something."

Roman wanted to be filled in on what we were talking about. I now realized that all of my friends looked at me as if I were the big bad wolf. "Anyway." I change the subject and turned to face Roman. "If you ever call yourself sneaking in my bedroom again, I would get off for killing you, ya know!"

Roman started laughing before he replied. "You just mad because I caught you off guard and found out you were lying."

"Lying 'bout what?" Quincy had to know.

"Man, when she was over yesterday, she shut down all action saying it was because her "friend" was in town."

"Oh shit, is she cute?" Everyone at the table looked at Quincy as if he was Cole on Martin.

"Man… I'm not even going to answer that."

Quincy started laughing. "Nigga, I ain't stupid. You the one sitting over there sounding like a chick talking 'bout "*her friend*." Quincy opens his chocolate milk and took a few gulps.

"Um, can we please stop talking about this? You guys are so gross, I swear! Aren't you supposed to be in detention or something Q?" I take a bite of my hamburger and toss it onto my tray.

Quincy waves me off. "Man whatever, Mr. Morrison ain't even here today. Sub don't know shit."

"So, Roman… you give anymore thought to what I said?" Hunter leans towards Roman.

"Doubt it… I don't even remember what you said."

"Oh, yeah!" Quincy scoots his chair in closer and they both act as if Roman was a celebrity they couldn't wait to touch.

I already know what Roman is thinking so I hurry and speak for him. "Uh no! Scavengers! He already told y'all he is not throwing no game. Now leave it alone and back up!" I fan the air as if it would physically push both of them back.

"Whose lunch is this?" Roman asked as he lifted a few fries from the lunch tray.

"It's mine." Amber was back from the bathroom, helping herself to an empty seat at the table.

"Oh, man… my bad." Roman slides her tray towards her.

"It's okay. You can have some." Both Quincy and Roman grabbed at the invitation until only one fry remained.

It's okay. You can have some. Echoed in my head and annoyed the hell out of me for some reason. "Why y'all eat all her stuff like that?" I move Amber's tray closer to her. Not that I cared. I just didn't like the thought of Roman taking or eating anything thing she had to offer. This Frenemy thing is harder than I thought. It took all I had to do that chick's make-up. Thank God, I carry extra cotton balls and Q-tips. I wasn't using my stuff on her diseased face! I used the cotton balls for the foundation and the Q-tips to apply her lipstick, eye shadow, and anything else.

"She just said we could have some?" Quincy answers for both he and Roman.

"Some don't mean all! Plus she said Roman, not you Quincy!" Hunter wipes her mouth with a napkin as she smacked Quincy's hand and gave him a dirty look. Yup, she was probably thinking the same thing I was thinking. Hmmph… and she wanna call me thirsty and pressed!

"It's okay." Amber barely looked at anyone in particular. "I'm not very hungry anyway."

"Yeah, man… she said I could get some, not you." There was an awkward silence at the table until Quincy broke it.

"I see you got your face fixed." Hunter slaps Quincy on his shoulder to remind him of his manners.

"Symphony redid it for me." Amber peeps up at me and looks back down.

"Looks nice. I don't know what was wrong with it the first time." Roman licks his lips while he stares at Amber. She thanks him without looking up and I swear I just threw up in my mouth a lil bit.

I get out my cellphone to check my Facebook because this whole table was making me sick right about now. "Dang Quincy! Facebook stalker!" I blurt out. "I see you went through all my pics and liked 'em."

"Whatever. Don't get too happy. I was bored."

I snarl at Quincy. "Amber I can't seem to find your page."

"Oh, I don't have a Facebook." Everyone at the table looked at each other as if she had said something obscene.

"Why not?" Quincy asked.

"I don't have many friends, just Ryder and Willow. They don't have a Facebook either."

"Is you that damn shy? You need to get out of that." Roman spoke up.

I couldn't help but laugh out loud. "Roman you're stupid! Now who's picking on her?"

"Nah. I ain't pickin'. I'm just saying people that shy just miss out a lot on life because they're too scared to live and let go. I mean, (YOLO) You only live once, right?"

"Okay, maybe you should change your Facebook name to Roman Philosopher Davis." I place my cell phone back into my bag.

"Don't sleep. I just might." Roman pinched the tip of his chin as if he were seriously thinking about it. "So what's up? Y'all want to hit up skating this weekend?"

14 CHAPTER FOURTEEN

Roll Bounce

AMBER READ OR SAW a movie somewhere that men love to rescue damsels in distress. She had made plans on becoming that distressed damsel that Roman rescues tonight. She had it all planned out. Well, not really. She was going to ad-lib. Tonight, here at this skating rink, she was an actress, and was about to play the heck out of this part. The only thing that's messing her up right now, she needed make-up. She hadn't been able to get her hands on any as of yet, and she wasn't about to make that same mistake of using her mom's again. If she was lucky and played her cards right, maybe… just maybe Symphony will make her over like she did before at school. All she had to do was wash it off before her mom comes back to pick them up.

It took everything in her power to beg her mother to let her go skating, tonight. Amber's mother only agreed if she took Cam'Ron with her. But the truth of the matter was, Cam was still on punishment so it was even harder to get her mother to let them go. What was even harder than that, after she convinced her mom, was that Cam didn't want to go. Amber begged, coaxed, and made all types of deals with Cam, just for him to go.

"I can't believe we are finally here." Amber says to Willow.

Willow gives Amber the stank face and replies, "You act like we don't never come here." Willow gives the white guy working the counter her and Amber's shoe size.

"Yeah, but that's different. That's always with the youth group and our moms' as chaperones. How fun is that?" Amber looks around to see if see anybody from school. She sees the twins coming in the door and hurries to turn around so they couldn't see her.

"Best friend here." Willow hands Amber her skates and they sit down to put them on. "You keep staring around like Ms. Joi is going to come up in here and ruin your parade." They both laugh but that's only half true. Amber was looking for Roman and hoping her mom doesn't run up in there and confess she can't live without her, so she'll just sit and watch. Another reason was that she was trying to keep an eye on the twins before one of them sneak up on her with another right hook.

Cam'Ron comes and sits with Amber and Willow. "So what's up, Willow? When me and you goin' hook up?" Cam tries to place his arm around Willow's shoulder but she smacks it back as if they were playing tennis and it was her turn to serve.

"Boy please!"

"Oh, it's like that now?"

"It's been like that, Cam. Besides, you are too young."

Cam scoots a few inches away from Willow. "Ew, too young for what? I thought you was one of those nice girls. But I see the real Willow now… you one of those gutter girls!" Cam'Ron playfully pushes Willow away.

"Where are your skates?" Willow asks as she laces hers.

"Man, what I look like skatin' that's for fruity niggas… even the word sounds fruity."

The three of them laugh and Amber busts her brother out. "He's just mad because he can't skate." Amber looks down at Cam'Ron's feet. "Where you get those shoes from?"

"Damn, Amber… why you all up in mine?" Cam'Ron gets defensive and walks away.

It has been at least an hour and Amber has given up looking for Roman to come about 45 minutes ago. She lets loose and Willow and she were having fun acting like little kids, dancing and skating to the beat. Seeing that the twins seemed to have been preoccupied bullying someone else at the moment, Amber let loose and was jamming. "Ut oh! Watch out Willow! I'm 'bout to do it backwards!" Amber slides her foot, switches her body, and starts dancing and skating backwards.

WHAM! She slams right into someone and their skates are entangled. Amber just knows she's about to head face forward onto the ground. Hands grab around her waist and pull her in closer to their body. She feels whoever has grabbed her has kept her safe from a disaster. "It's all good. I got you, baby." She knew that smell. That touch. That feeling. Amber looks up and straight into Roman's face. She gets lost in his eyes and never want to look away. That is until she remembers that, she's not an actress nor is she one of those beautiful people. But her worse feeling is, she's not wearing any make-up. Amber began to feel sweat drip from her armpits. Her legs began to wobble. Those darn skates weren't helping much either. His touch and her touching him, sent Amber's insides into a quivering frenzy. It was that awkward moment when you weren't sure when or if you should break away from the touch or not. She wanted to hold onto Roman forever and she felt like she did, until she feels him loosening his grip so she does too.

"I see you were out there doing your thang!" Amber could tell he was smiling but she didn't dare look up at him. His comment made her wonder how long had he been here? Did he see Willow and her acting a fool? How was she to play the damsel in distress now when she don't know how much of her skating and dancing he saw?

"Why you here?" Symphony says to Amber as she skates to Roman and wraps her arms around his waist. It was as if Symphony had grabbed Amber's heart the same way and crushed it until it disintegrated into nothing but ashes. Amber gets it now. Roman is the fire hydrant and Symphony is the bitch that comes and pisses on him to mark her territory.

"I'm here with my friend Willow and my brother, Cam." Amber musters up enough courage to say as she points to Willow leaving the rink heading towards the bathroom.

"Whatever." Symphony grabs Roman's face and kisses him on the lips. She turns towards Amber and says, "Problem?"

Amber jolts back into reality because she had no idea she was standing there in the middle of the rink staring at the two of them kissing. Symphony shoves Amber a bit and tells her to go skate. "Isn't that what you came here for?"

Amber rolls toward the flowing crowd almost tripping, but before she can gather her balance, the twins' wiz past and elbows her. "Dang! Move out the way, you seen the professionals coming through." The wheels on Amber's skates entangle each other and she falls face first.

"My dang finger is killing me! I can't believe that "B" did that. That just shows me how threatening she thinks I am. I'm glad Roman was there to rescue me from my first fall." Amber says to Willow who was in the bathroom mirror fiddling with her hair.

Amber thinks as she waits for a response from Willow. *I may have to rethink my strategy. I could tell he don't like the dummy shy role. He must like smart girls or something. I can do smart."*

"Amber, you're tripping." Willow finally says.

"But I just can't stand the thought of letting symphony and them twins get the best of me like that! They need to get some payback for that mess."

"You need to just turn the other cheek and be the bigger person. You know that."

"Hmmm... The way I see it, I'm a giant right now with no cheeks! I've been letting people take advantage of me, use me, and make fun of me. Hmm, I think it's time for Amber Styles to start fighting back!"

"I see now the real reason why you were dying to come tonight." Willow washes her hands in the sink. "No wonder you couldn't wait until Youth Sunday."

I swear to God this chick be acting like me and her go together. "So what if that's my real reason for wanting to come here. You need to lighten up Willow, fo-real."

"And you need to smarten up Amber." Amber's facial expression asked Willow what the heck she meant by that and she continues. "You had me thinking that Roman wants you. He don't care nothing about you!"

Ouch! Amber's best friend was slicing through her skin with a butcher knife and pouring sea salt into the wounds.

Willow thinks she knows everything! She even think she's smarter than me when it comes to the Bible because she be getting all the questions right in Bible study. Shoot she should! Her mama's the Bible study teacher! She probably knows all the questions and the answers before we even start. Amber thinks as she ignores Willow's attempt at wisdom and felt she was more experienced because Willow hasn't even kissed a boy like she has. Well, it was just Ryder. And it was just a peck. It still counts though. Ryder asked Willow first but she turned him down saying it was a sin if you didn't really love the person enough to marry them.

Amber tells Willow, "Help me come up with a plan?"

She says, "Unh unh... I don't want no parts of this mess."

"What kind of friend are you that can't even have my back?"

"I am your friend! That's why I'm trying to steer you into the right direction. I got yo back."

"Yeah... Way back!"

"Come on."

"Where?"

"I want you to introduce me to your knew found friends and then maybe you will see that I know what I'm talking about."

Amber didn't have a problem with proving her wrong, she was looking forward to it. They both reached the table where Roman, Symphony, Quincy, and Spirit were all sitting at eating snacks.

"Hey." Amber says to no one in particular. "This is my friend, Willow."

"Hello, Amber's friend, Willow." Roman shakes Willow's hand and Amber felt that Willow got a little happy from touching her man's hand.

"Sup." Quincy said more engrossed inside of his bag of chips than looking up at who he was greeting.

"Yeah, I already know her. We go to the same church." Spirit waved at Willow.

"Since when you go to church?" Quincy said as he emptied the last bit of chips into his mouth.

"Shut up Q!" Spirit shot back as she was untying her laces so she could give her feet a rest from the smelly skates.

It had got quiet after that and started to get awkward so Amber said, "Where's Hunter at?"

"She where she at, nosey—"

"Symphony please… dang!" Roman interrupted her.

"She couldn't make it." Quincy spoke without looking at Amber.

"Thank you Quincy. I appreciate the answer." Amber looks at the clock on the wall and grabs Willow by the arm to make it seem like she really wanted to get some skating in before it was time for them to go. Amber knew by the limited responses that it was her que to exit stage left before someone makes a bigger butt out of her in front of Willow.

♥♥♥

Roman uses a urinal next to Cam'Ron and looks over at him. "What? Is you gay?" Cam zips up and washes his hands.

"I'm just wondering when you were going to finish?" Roman washes his hands too and wait for Cam'Ron to respond.

"Finish what?"

"Pulling your pants up. You know all that saggin' stuff started in prison, right? It was to let other men know they were "available" or looking for a "boyfriend." Cam'Ron turns his back to Roman ignoring him but Roman grabs his arm and turns him back around. "I'm trying to teach you something."

Cam'Ron looks Roman up and down and distorts his face. "Yeah, just like I thought… gay! Anybody that thinks about saggin' like that is gay. Yea, I'll give you that… Saggin' did actually originate in the prison system but not for the reasons you say. In most jails, you ain't allowed to have no belts because corny niggas be committing suicide and ish and them niggas don't give a damn if your stuff fits you correctly or not. Ergo, saggin' was born. So you ain't trying to teach me shit!"

"What's your problem, huh?" Roman was literally confused on why Cam'Ron was hating him when he's barely had a conversation with him.

"You my problem! I don't even see why my sister be crushin' on you. You's a soft ass nigga. You ain't even old enough to teach me nothing… I got a daddy… where's yours? Matt-o-fact… where yo mama, nigga?"

Roman laughs a little, bites his lip, and sticks his fingertips into his jean pockets, deciding to ignore every comment Cam'Ron just made except the part about him being soft. "How you figure that?"

"I saw you running the other day from Patrón and Remy."

"Is that right? Because I can't recall running from anybody or anything."

"Oh, that's right… I guess the word you would prefer to use is, "avoiding." Roman waved Cam'Ron off because he felt he was fighting a losing battle. Why should he care if this little dude sags or not. He wasn't his brother or even in his squad, so later for him. Roman leaves Cam'Ron in the bathroom bent down tying his shoes.

"Them some hot ass sneakers."

"Yeah I know." Cam answers without looking up as he wipes a smudge off his shoes. He stares down at the two pair of shoes as another pair of smaller ones joins them. Cam'Ron hears a lighter flick and within minutes he could smell marijuana filling the air. He looks up into Remy's face. Then at Patrón. And then Christian who was their younger brother.

"So where you get them sneakers from, Homie?" Remy speaks as he's holding in the smoke at the same time.

"I-I bought these." Cam'Ron stutters. Somehow when he was walking past their apartment and saw the package with the Finishline label, he really didn't think anyone would miss the shoes that were inside the box. He thought that maybe they'd just order another pair or whatever. Cam'Ron never really thought they would figure out it was him.

"Is that right? What kind of job you got at 13? You slangin'?" Patrón steps closer to Cam'Ron… a little too close for comfort, Cam'Ron felt.

"M-my momma bought these for me."

"Really?" Patrón turns to Remy and says, "Bruh… we got the wrong person. I think we need to be talkin' to his moms right about now. What you think?"

"D-don't d-do that!" Cam'Ron had heard stories about Remy and Patrón not caring who or how they confront anyone. Not even someone's parents.

"Hmm… it's mighty funny how we just ordered Lil Man here those same exact sneakers. For some reason, we never got the order, although the tracking says we did!"

Cam'Ron was beginning to shake, if he hadn't already relieved himself he might have peed his pants right now. Patrón and Remy both grabbed each one of his arms so that Cam'Ron's midsection was exposed.

"You know them my Jordans!" Christian jabs Cam'Ron in his stomach as hard and as many times as his medium sized fist could handle.

"It's a few things we don't like." Remy butts out his blunt. "A thief and a liar." Remy and Patrón released Cam'Ron. Remy lifted and distorted his voice up a few octaves to sound like a white man. "And you sir, are both!" Remy kept his eyes on Cam'Ron but spoke to his younger brother at the same time. "Lil' Man?"

"Wassup?"

"This nigga here, stole your Jordans and lied to you in your face."

"True."

"What you want to do? You want them shoes back?"

"Hell naw… they used now."

"I know that's right!" Patrón chimed in. "So you just goin' let him have them?"

"Is Jordan's water? Cause ain't nothing free. You take from a Walker, you goin' have to pay!"

Remy and Patrón stood watching as Christian beat the crap out of Cam'Ron's face as if it were a punching bag. Cam'Ron balls his fist with the intentions of fighting back until Patrón steps in and says, "What you plan on doing with those? You even think about touching my brother and it's goin' be me and you! And don't think we forgot about you putting your hands on my lil sis." Cam'Ron tries to stand up straight and take the hits like a man. To Cam'Ron, it wasn't about learning his lesson and not steal again. In his mind, he was thinking the ass kicking was worth owning a pair of $200 Jordans.

"You still in here?" Roman walks back into the bathroom and sees Christian beating Cam'Ron while Patrón and Remy watched. "Yo, what the hell?' Roman runs to help Cam'Ron up, but not before they removed the Jordans from Cam'Ron's feet.

Roman grabs toilet paper from the roll and held it up to Cam'Ron's nose. He looks over at Patrón, Remy, and Christian who are now urinating inside of the Jordans. "Aye! What y'all doing?"

"We can piss in my shoes if we want too." Christian laughs as he continues to fill the inside of the shoe.

"Put 'em back on." Patrón was dead serious when he spoke to Cam'Ron.

"What? You can't be that fowl?" Roman spoke for Cam'Ron.

"Oh we can… and we is." Lil Man said. "Now put 'em on!" He tried his best to mimic that of his older brother.

Cam'Ron uses the wall to stand, walks toward the shoes, and then looks back at Roman. He raises one foot and stops in midair when he hears Roman say, "Y-you don't have to do that Cam'Ron." Roman grabs Cam by his arm.

"Yeah, you don't have to do it, Cam'Ron." Remy imitates Roman and glares into Cam's eyes. Cam'Ron already knew what was up. He snatches his arm away from Roman and sink his left foot into one of the Jordans. His foot soaked up the urine like a sponge. Cold and wet, Cam'Ron stuck his other foot into the second shoe.

Laughter rang out. "Ew, you's a nasty nigga." Little Man said as he pointed at Cam'Ron. Cam'Ron held his head up high, so high it was as if his chin was pointing at the three of them. Oh yeah, Cam'Ron wanted to cry but he didn't dare. Not in front of the Walkers and dang sure not in front of Roman. He looks at the smug face Christian wore and wondered how in the world they were ever friends.

Remy headed for the bathroom door with his brothers tagging along. "I want to see you in those shoes you stole from my brother every day for the next two months. If there's even one day that I or one of my brother's see you without those Jordans on… Well, let's just say, it won't be as nice as it was today.

15 CHAPTER FIFTHTEEN
SYMPHONY PERKINS
I.O.U.

I HAD BEEN GONE the majority of the day, running around trying to get someone to purchase my latest pieces for a decent price. Some people can be so cheap sometimes. How am I supposed to make a profit if every time I turn around, someone's expecting a "You my girl! You know I'm good for it!" discount. Please! I can't buy nothing with an I.O.U…. so I don't see why they should from me.

I get in the house and grab a cold bottled water from the fridge. I pause when I notice that dishes are in the sink from earlier this morning. That was definitely not like Melody. There's peanut butter and jelly dripped and smeared on the countertop and the loaf of bread is wide open. I see a chair up against the counter which means Harmony must have fixed herself something to eat. It was odd to me because Melody would usually do it for her to avoid the extra mess.

I walk upstairs to check on Harmony. She's in her room watching a DVD of Frozen and singing along. "Do you want to build a snowmaaaaan…".

"Hey boo, where's mommy?

"She sleepin'."

"She been sleep all day?"

"Yes… no… I dunno." She goes back to watching Frozen as she stuffs the end of her sandwich into her mouth and prances around the room as if she was Anna.

Even though it's still daylight, Melody's room is pitch black. She has her curtains closed and a blanket is thrown over the rod. I yank the blanket down and open the curtains to let the sun beat down onto her face. She shrieks at the sight of light like a vampire. "What are you doing?"

"How long have you been in bed?"

"Why? She uses her arms to shield her eyes from the light.

"Because the house is a mess! You have Harmony fending for herself while you just lay here!"

"She's fine!" Melody snatches the covers away from her and jumps out of bed. Her hair is in cornrows. That's the way she usually wears it under her wigs. Nothing special just braided straight back. She yanks the curtains closed and pushes me toward her bedroom door. "Clean it up then! What do you do around here anyway besides prancing in the mirror?" She jumps back in bed and pulls the covers over her head.

I clutch the covers and for a minute we wrestle with them until she gives up. "When were you going to tell me?"

"Tell you what?"

"About our money situation."

"What money situation?"

I stood there and purse my lips for a moment because I couldn't believe that she was going to sit there and straight up play me like I'm stupid to my face. "I seen the bank statement, Melody. We had ten-thousand dollars left in the bank. I'm sure it's probably less now."

"Why is you all up in my business?"

"Because, your business is my business. It affects me too and don't think for one minute I'm going back into modeling! I saw the pamphlets."

"Who said the pamphlets were for you? How do you figure that when you haven't worked for anything that's in my bank account? That little money you did model for is long gone!"

"Last I checked, there was no way you could have worked for it either?"

Melody shakes her head. "Nope, not having this conversation with you unless you're trying to be adult enough to help rectify the situation."

"So now you're admitting that there is a situation?"

"What? No, there is no situation, if there was or will be I'll make sure to let you know because you're the mother not me, obviously." She grabs the covers and place them back over her head.

I shake her. "Mother, if money isn't the problem so you say, then what is?"

"Symphony! I have a migraine, now shut up and leave me alone!"

Yeah right, migraine my behind. Melody is stressing just like I am and like she said, it's not even my problem. I'm sure she's having some type of man problems. She tends to get like that if one of her dudes stop calling, don't give her any money, or say they're not leaving their wives.

♥♥♥

I've been having a real hard time trying to be cordial with Amber but I don't know. It's just something about her that just rubs me the wrong way. Just looking at her makes my skin crawl. Every time I try to be nice to her, my aspirations, just jumps ship and abort all operations.

I've been doing kind of good for the past few weeks. I still haven't helped her with any of her damn make-up though. Every time I turn around, she's begging me to redo her jacked up face! See, that's why you can't be nice to people. Once you do it, they expect it all the time! And then you find yourself in a use me situation. I'm not about to be used, by nobody. Especially not her!

Ok, y'all making me get all roweled up again. Let me calm down… whoosa…..

"Did you go get fitted for your tux yet?" I admit, I love to see the look on Amber's face when I bring up relationship stuff between Roman and me. Not only can she not conceal those bumps on her face… neither can she conceal her jealousy.

"Tux?"

"Duh, for Winter Formal?"

"I gotta wear a tux for Winter Formal? Why not just a suit?"

"No! I let you wear a suit last year. Do you remember how you looked?"

Roman laughed, "You let me?"

"Yeah… I let you!" He know I let him. Why he trying to front for everybody.

"We still got time. Winter Formal is a ways off from now."

"Maybe for you it is but not when you are designing a Designer Original by Symphony Sew Unique!"

"Wow!" Amber's mouth was wide open. "You make your own clothes? Did you like take classes for that?"

"Girl no! Meesha taught me!"

"Who's that?" Amber wanted to know.

"YouTube. Look her up. DIYMEESHA. If you ever wanted to sew but don't know how, she's definitely the one to show you how to sew easy."

"Bae, you okay?" Roman asked me that because he knew how touchy this subject was for me. I don't understand how someone could take someone else's life like that. She had so much potential and helped so many people. I didn't even personally know her but I loved her just the same and cried my eyes out when I logged on to find no new post but horrible news that she would never make a post again.

"I'm fine." I change my thoughts and turn to Hunter. "Hunter when are you going to come back over for a fitting?"

"I don't know yet."

"What's wrong with you?" For some reason she seemed to have major stankness coming from her way.

"There's nothing wrong with me. Why do something have to be wrong with me?"

Ok. I know she my girl and she tired. I'm going to chalk it up to being just that. I'm not even going to respond. Right now… I'm going to let the Winter Formal thing go.

We had about five minutes until the lunch period was over and a few hours away until the weekend.

"But fo-real though." Roman began to place his trash on his tray. "Y'all want to hit up the movies tonight? About 10pm?"

Quincy and I were the only ones who said yeah. Amber just sat their quietly like a bump on the log. Hunter said, "Can't."

"Why not?" Quincy looked at Hunter.

"Because my mom works tonight and I have to watch my brothers."

"Can't yo dad watch 'em?"

"Yeah, but he can't watch my little brother Josiah. He's only a few months old Quincy."

Symphony chimed in. "I can't believe your mom had another baby."

"What's that supposed to mean?"

"Oh, Hunter get your panties out ya butt, I'm just saying."

"Saying what?"

Again, I could see that this conversation was going nowhere, because right now, I was doing all I could, not to come across that table and whoop Hunter's sarcastic ass.

"Aight y'all chill out and put yo cat claws back in. Hunter I'm sure she didn't mean nothing by it." Roman stood up and grabbed his tray. "If not today, we'll figure out something to do this weekend?"

I place my tray on top of Roman's so he could throw my trash away. "Come on Amber, walk me to my locker." As much as I hated to say it, I had to get away from Hunter right now. That girl's funky attitude was about to make me blow a fuse.

16 CHAPTER SIXTEEN
AMBER STYLES
Mmm…Mmm… Good

WHEN I LOOK AT Quincy I think.... Hmmm... He cute. He on the basketball team, play football for Westbrook. Popular as heck. Yeah, I could get with that.

But when I look at Roman... Mmm mmm ... Roman. Just the sound of his name gives me goose bumps. When I look at him, I really be looking at him. Not just about the way he look or the sports he plays. It's like I can look into his soul and know he was made for me. It's just the certain way I feel when I'm around him. I want to marry him, make him my husband, and even have a few kids by him. I feel like I would do anything for him. Heck, he makes me want to lose any bit of religion I do have.

I was more than happy when Symphony asked me to walk with her to her locker. I couldn't wait to get away from Roman. Even though I was crushing on him big time, the pressure of being in his presence was too much for me to bear.

I had to figure out how to get to the movies with Roman. Shoot, I still haven't found me a date for Winter Formal. Symphony has obviously made it apparent that she has her claws in Roman. Looks like Hunter and Quincy are going together, but she just seems like she could care less. But right now, that was the least of my problems. No way was my mom going to let me go, especially not at 10 o'clock at night.

Symphony told me she didn't want to be the only girl, I didn't blame her. I wouldn't want to be the only girl either. Just like Symphony said, I owed her from when she did my make-up that time. I would do anything in my power to make good on what she did for me. Shoot, I'm just hoping she will do my make-up again. I be asking her to do it again, but she always blows me off. I feel like I'm a crack-feign and she holds my rocks. But the way I figure, I ain't going keep on asking… I'll get me some sooner or later.

On the real though, I had to level with Symphony and tell her the truth on how strict my mom was and that spending the night with her would be out of the question.

"Well, what if I came over to meet your mom? She might let you spend the night then?"

I hated to disappoint Symphony even though I knew she secretly hated me. I couldn't help but think, if I do this one thing, then maybe… just maybe… we might be cool in some sort of weird way. I was at a loss for words on what to tell Symphony without sounding lame.

"No worries." Symphony grabs the books she needed for her next classes. "Where there's a will, there's always a way. I'll tell the guys to maybe push it back till tomorrow or something."

"Okay, cool." I still didn't know what to say or how to even respond. All I knew was I was going to have to come up with a master plan that somehow involved Willow. At the moment, me and her were on silent terms again. It didn't matter though, she knows she can't go more than a day without talking to me.

"Hand me your phone so I can put my number in it." Symphony held her hand out waiting for my cell phone.

There was no way I was going to tell her I didn't have a phone. "I-I must have forgotten it at home." I felt my back pockets and fiddled around inside my purse.

Symphony raised her left eyebrow higher than the other. "Yeah, okay… hmm." She held out her cell handing it to me. Instead of grabbing it, I stared at it like it was a foreign object. "You don't even have a damn cell, do you?"

I reluctantly shook my head no.

"Liar." Symphony laughed and placed her cell back into her purse. "Once you start a lie, you're supposed to stick to it, dummy."

♥♥♥

After Praise Dance practice, it was a piece of cake sucking back up to Willow and Ryder. If I had my way, I wouldn't have even talked to Ryder with that stunt he pulled a while ago. But what was I to do, he came with the territory.

So far, the plan that I had conjured up, was to spend the weekend with Willow. I didn't know what else I was going to do after that, nor did I have a plan B. This scheming and conniving thing was new to me and I wasn't sure if I was comfortable with it. One thing was for certain, letting the squad down, weren't an option.

I had talked Willow into helping me coax my mother into letting me spend the night; which wasn't hard to do because Willow was all too excited. It had been a while since I had spent the night and Willow thought this would be a nice time to hang out like old times, pop some popcorn, and watch reruns. Nevertheless, to my dismay, my mother wasn't budging.

"No, Amber, I thought you and I would spend some time together tonight."

"Aw, c'mon ma!" I begged giving my mom my best puppy dog eyes.

"Are you wearing make-up?" My mom said inspecting my face.

Oh I forgot, in good faith, Symphony did a rush job on my face before we headed to class. She just covered my dark spots really quick with foundation, some eyeliner, and a shot of the troublemaker lipstick. I have to say, I am loving that lipstick.

"What? No!" I shook my face away from my mom's hands.

"Well, it looks like you tried to put on some eyeliner or something." I gave my mom the… 'You know, I know, better' look'.

Please believe that as soon as I made it home, I ran into the bathroom to wash my face. Symphony's liquid liner was the hardest, so yeah, my mom might've saw some faint traces of liner.

My mom told me to wrap it up and she will be outside in the church parking lot waiting. She did however say that maybe tomorrow I could spend the night at Willows because she had to work late.

"If I was you, I would run straight to the alter right now and repent." Willow whispered into my ear.

"For what?"

"All those l-l-lies you just told to your m-m-mom." Ryder butted in.

"I ain't tell no lie. If you were listening carefully, her question was, are you wearing make-up? And I simply said no, because technically I'm not because I had washed it off.

"Yeah okay. Play word games with God if you want to. You'll be burning in the fiery pits of hell." Willow slid her feet inside her shoes. "So what do you want to do tomorrow if your mom lets you spend the night?"

"I dunno. I guess we'll have to play it by ear."

♥♥♥

I lay there in the dark watching my curtains blowing from a nice breeze. My room had a nice glow from the street lights outside. I tried to work on my plans in my head when I heard a hissing sound coming from outside. I didn't know what it was so I tried ignore it but it was hard because all I could do was focus on a dark figure coming from behind my pink curtains.

I opened my mouth to scream for my mom but nothing came out. I was frozen stiff with my eyes locked on the dark shadow approaching.

Then something moved my curtains back and whispered, "PSST… Amber." More light illuminated into my room as a car went down the street. I slowly eased over to my bedroom door and cracked it closed. I couldn't close it all the way because believe me my mom would know. I went in front of the window and sat on the floor.

"Quincy? What are you doing here?" My heart was beating overtime for a few reasons, one, I was almost scared to death, two I couldn't believe this dude was here at my window at 11:00 PM, and three I didn't want my mom to catch me.

"Sup baby girl?" Quincy flashed his smile exposing his slightly chipped front tooth.

"Symphony wanted us to come by. Said she forgot to exchange numbers with you for the plans tomorrow."

WOW! I couldn't believe this. I was wondering how I was going to get in touch with Symphony. "Wait, you said us… is she here?"

"Nope, I am."

OMG! I think I just peed my jammies a little. I was about to melt like butter when I saw Roman. I mean, Quincy had me feeling like margarine in the fridge. It's only soft a little. But Roman, I was like melted butter in a microwave set for sixty minutes on a hot summer's day when it was like 100 degrees outside.

"Why we whispering?"

"'Cause my mom's in the other room."

Quincy pulled his head further into the window. "Let me see what you got on. Stand up."

I was about to stand up when Roman pushed Quincy out the way. "You ain't gotta' listen to that nigga."

"Aye, where your pops at?" Quincy and Roman fought to share a spot at my window.

"I dunno. Home I guess." Then a thought occurred to me. "How did you guys know where I lived, let alone which window was mine?"

They both started laughing and I freaked. "Shhhhh! Y'all going to wake up my mom and get me in trouble!" I went towards the door to make sure I could still hear the faint snoring of my mom.

"Nah man! I'm a tell you what happened, right." Roman licked his fine lips as he continued to speak. "We've been here for a minute, right. And this nigga had first looked into your mom's window.

"Damn! Man, how old is your mom's 'cause she is bangin'!" they laughed themselves away from the window this time so it wouldn't echo inside of my room.

"Dude, was you spying on my mom?"

"I couldn't help it. Why don't you hook me up with your mom's for real though?" Quincy asked this time looking serious.

"Eww! Are you serious?"

"Hell yeah! Why… you don't think I can hit that?"

"Man, get yo ass out of here." Roman pushed Quincy out the way.

"Amber? I know you ain't on my phone this late at night are you? And do you have your door closed?"

I jumped into my bed and Quincy and Roman disappeared. I hopped back out of my bed and fell crashing to the floor with a loud thump because my feet had become entangled in my sheets.

"What the hell are you doing?"

"Ah, nothing." I was sure I was about to have a heart attack because this night was more excitement than I'd ever had in my life. I crack my door open a little.

"All the way, Amber. And you and Willow stay off my damn phone, it's almost midnight!"

"Okay Ma!" I open my bedroom door all the way and climb back in bed. I smile to myself, thinking of Roman and Quincy at my window. Me of all people. I couldn't wait to throw this in Willow's face. Then my heart plunged all the way down to my belly. I grab my stomach and rub it, feeling a bout of the bubble guts coming on. In the mist of all the excitement, I'd forgotten to give them my phone number for Symphony to call me.

My pity party was short lived because I couldn't contain my happiness. I had to do something to express myself. I couldn't jump on the bed, because the squeak from it would be too loud. I climb out of bed and decide to quietly do a happy dance from the floor. I squeeze my eyes shut and wail my arms in the air and whip my head back and forth. I could do this all night, and then I break out into the Carlton.

As I twirl around toward the window, I open my eyes and see Roman standing there staring at me. Again! How does he always pop up when I'm doing something crazy and embarrassing? I wondered if he'd been there the whole time. I was so humiliated I cover my face with my hands. When I look up again, Roman put his thumb and pinky finger to his ears reminding me of the phone number.

I jot my number down on a scrap piece of paper and hand it to him. Roman lick his lips and whisper, "Is this for me?"

Saying that I cheesed from ear to ear was an understatement. I wanted to be bold enough to grab Roman by the face and plant one of the biggest most sensual kisses on his lips. I often fantasized about romantic things I'd seen in a movie. I move in closer to the window and smile.

"Why are you in the window!?"

My head flung around to meet my mom's stare in the doorway. A few drops of pee really did escape my body this time. I stood there speechless and motionless. What is she? A freakin' nosey vampire! Why don't she go to sleep!

"If you're that hot, turn your fan on." My mom walked completely into my room and clicked my fan on. I looked back at the window but Roman was already gone. I didn't know whether to thank God or declare my mother my nemesis.

I place my hands over my heart to feel how fast my heart was beating. I try to shift more weight to my feet in order to make my legs stop shaking. I couldn't believe what a close call that was.

"Close your window. You don't want too much air on you." My mom went back to bed and I walk over to the window to close it, but not before sticking my head out to search for Roman. He was slowly walking down my driveway. He looks back and smile. I smiled back.

17 CHAPTER SEVENTEEN
HUNTER SANTOS

Don't be fooled by their mask. Fake people eventually show their true colors. Just wait until their mask needs cleaning.

IT WAS 3AM AND Josiah looks as if he was up to stay and ready to play. It was nights like this, I wished my mother didn't have to work, especially nights. I lie Josiah on the bed and grab his bag of diapers to get ready to change him. It was only one diaper left. This was not going to last him until 8:00 in the morning.

I started searching the house and his diaper bag for more, but no luck. The one diaper would have to suffice and I would have to cross that bridge when I got to it.

After changing Josiah's diaper, I ran into the kitchen to fill up his bottle and of course there wasn't any formula left either. I filled Josiah's bottle with tap water hoping that it would satisfy him until I could get more Simalac.

I dreaded going into Papi's room to wake him, but Josiah needed his essentials and there was no other way around it. I tried to feed him the water but it only worked for a millisecond. Josiah began to cry and fidget.

I stand at my parents' bedroom door staring into the blackness and calling out to my father. "Papi." I call him a few more times before turning on the lights to find the room empty.

I look out the window but his car wasn't in the driveway. I dial his cell phone a few times but it went straight to voicemail. I was beginning to panic, not because my father wasn't here because he did that from time to time. Bothering my mother at work, was not a choice for me. I didn't want to stress her out any more than I already had.

I text Quincy a few times to see if he'd text me back but he didn't. I don't blame him; it was after three in the morning.

Josiah didn't want the water or his binky. I knew he wanted his milk and could tell he was getting hungry. I swallow hard and dial Roman's cell but he didn't answer either.

I sit on the edge of my bed holding onto Josiah. I rock back and forth until tears began to stream down my face. I feel so alone right now, as if nobody in this world gave a damn about me. The more I cry, the louder Josiah cried.

My cell began to chime and I pick it up without checking the caller ID. "Hello?" I sniffle into the receiver.

"Hey…" there was a pause in the caller's voice. "What's wrong? Everything okay?"

"No!" My sniffling burst into crying again, when I hear Roman's voice.

"Calm down…" There was shuffling over the phone as if Roman was trying to reposition himself. "Tell me what's wrong?" His caring tone began to soothe me and I try to explain my situation to him the best I could.

"Okay, so you need some milk and diapers?" Roman began to sound more awake.

"Yeah."

"What kind?"

"It doesn't matter." I knew that beggars couldn't be choosey.

"Babe, I ain't never bought no milk or diapers before, so you're going to have to help me out here." He laughs a little but I could tell that he was sleepy and tired.

I explained to him what to get and he was knocking on my door in less than twenty minutes. When I see him standing there, I just wanted to hug him for coming to my rescue.

"Them other rugrats still sleep?" Roman asked referring to my little brothers. He followed me into the kitchen and sat the bag on the kitchen table.

"Yes, thank God!" I was still rocking Josiah trying to keep him calm.

Roman touched my face. "You look tired as hell."

"Thanks a lot."

"I don't mean it like that." Roman lifts up the container of Similac. "The lady at the store said you didn't have to do anything to this one. Whatever that means. But I got you the can ones too."

I started to cry all over again and my eyes were so puffy they looked as if they were swollen.

"No… no… no! Don't do that. Shhhh." Roman used his fingers to wipe away the already fallen tears from my face. "Hand me the baby and you do whatever you got to do with all that stuff there." He points to the milk on the table.

I used the already made Similac and pour it into a clean bottle for Josiah. When I had gotten to my room, Roman was spread out on my bed with Josiah fast asleep on his chest.

"How'd you do that?"

"I got the magic touch." That made me smile and even giggle a little. I walk over to get Josiah and lay him in his crib. "No… don't touch him." Roman swat my hands away. "He cool right now. Lock the door and come lay down. I wouldn't want your daddy running up on me with my eyes closed.

I lock my bedroom door and lie down on the other side of Roman and Josiah. Even though Roman had his eyes closed, it was hard for me to close mine. I kept having vision of Josiah rolling off Roman and onto the floor. "Maybe I should just put him in his crib?"

"What is you scared about?" Roman opens one eye and looked at me. "Here, would you feel better if I put your brother on this pillow between us?"

It did make me a little more comfortable but as soon as I closed my eyes, they popped back opened. "You're not going to tell Symphony about this are you?"

"Now why would I do that? You must think I'm crazy." Roman closed his eyes again. "Now go to sleep 'cause I got a feeling he'll be waking up soon."

For a moment, looking at Roman and Josiah sleep, life seemed pretty peaceful. I close my eyes and finally slept.

♥♥♥

"What time did you get home?!"

I open my eyes to Mami yelling. I jerk when I didn't see Josiah or Roman in the bed. For a split second I wondered if it were all a dream but it didn't account for why I still didn't see Josiah in his crib.

I jump up and search his crib, even lifting up the thin layer of his blanket as if he would be under there. My mind was running a mile a minute. Did Roman steal my baby brother? I drop to the floor crushing my kneecaps against the hardwood floor. I look under the bed to see if Josiah had fallen and rolled under the bed. Nothing! I began to panic. I had searched every inch of this room and still came up with nothing. I had become a raging mad woman.

I didn't bother to knock on my arguing parents' door, I just barged in. I looked inside. Nothing. For a split second, my parents stopped arguing and looked at me as if I was crazy.

I ran into the living room and without thinking, I snatch Josiah from

Justin's arms. "What do you think you're doing!?" I was a mad mama bear protecting her cub.

"I was feeding him!"

"We'll don't!" I snap at my brother, which made Josiah scream.

"He's not just yours ya know! He's my brother too!"

I knew I was wrong for snatching Josiah away from Justin like that but at that moment, I wasn't thinking clearly. I was running on fumes of adrenaline.

"What's going on in here?" My mother ran into the living room. "Give the baby back to Justin so you can get some sleep. Your eyes are all puffy."

"Okay." I calm myself down and gave Josiah back to Justin and went back into my room to lie down.

I started wondering what time Roman had left and if anyone had seen him. I wanted to call or text him because I don't remember if I had thanked him or not. I dial his number and he picks up on the second ring.

"Why are you calling my man's phone?" Symphony didn't say hello or anything, just straight to the third degree.

"Well hello to you too!" I said with a playful tone trying to sound as innocent and naive as I could. She didn't respond. But I did hear her breathing into the receiver. "I was looking for you." I lied.

"How is that when you haven't even attempted to dial my number or even text me, Hunter?" I had no excuse or reason I could give her. "And I see you called around 3am this morning!"

"Dang! You all in his phone ain't you?"

"You damn right!" She popped her gum in my ear. "So what the hell you want?"

"What is you doin'?" I hear Roman ask her from the background. "She was looking for Q. Why else would she be calling me?

"I don't know. You tell me."

I left them to argue amongst themselves and hung up the phone because my mother walked into my room and sat on the edge of my bed. "Hey, are you okay?"

"I'm fine." I turn and see Papi standing in the doorway.

"You were probably up with Josiah all night again, huh?"

I looked at my father and wondered if my parents were trying to catch me in some type of trap. "Y-yeah." I hesitated.

Papi continued to stand in the doorway not saying a word with his arms folded across his chest. The way he looked, I was sure he'd had a run in with Roman after seeing him in my bed.

"I hate to ask you this, but…" My mother paused before she finished her question.

"Mami, I can explain—"I know I was about to hear it now. What was I supposed to do? I don't have a car and I couldn't get a hold of either of them. I know I was wrong on so many levels having Roman in my bed, but I couldn't just throw him back on the street when he was already tired and the only living soul who helped me.

"Let your mother finish!" Papi barked interrupting my mid-confession.

"Explain what?" My mother looked at me quizzically and then at my father.

"Just ask her!"

"Was Papi home, last night?"

♥♥♥

OCTOBER

18 CHAPTER EIGHTEEN
GAME DAY
Westbrook Tigers vs. Cedarville Cougars

THIS DAY WAS AN important day for the Tigers and the Cougars. Both teams were undefeated with ranks of 4 & 0 for the season. This game was not just an ordinary game because whoever wins it will move on to the championship.

Roman Davis was considered MVP of the Westbrook Tigers. No games were won if Roman wasn't in it playing on every play. It was easy for Quincy Garnett to say he'll throw the game because his main position was watching from the sideline.

One-point two seconds left in the quarter before half-time. Number twenty-four from the Cougars overthrows the ball to the in zone and Roman catches it creating an interception. With only seconds to go, Roman spikes the ball in celebration completely unaware that the whistle hasn't blown and the ball is still in play. A Cougar sneaks up from behind grabs the ball and makes a touchdown! The whistle blows alerting everyone that the time has completely run out and it was now half-time. Each team runs off the field in opposite directions. The score was 20-27 in the favor of the Cougars.

"Psst yo!" Quincy grabs Roman by the arm and leads him over toward the sound of Remy's voice. "You know, at first I was kind of trippin' right?" Roman removes his helmet and squirts his water bottle over his head in an attempt to cool off. "But then after my cousin picked up that live ball and went right through you and scored that last touchdown, I knew you were a true game player. For that, seeing that it's half-time, half now… half later." Remy handed out a wad of cash in Roman's direction.

Roman ignored Remy and his money and jogged off to join the rest of his team. Quincy however didn't hesitate to grab the money and let Remy know that he'd split it up with Roman. Remy and Patrón both shook their heads at the site of Quincy's thirstiness. "We 'bout to bounce. We'll swing back around and pick y'all up later." He gave the other wad of cash which was a thousand dollars to his twin sisters. "Handle that at the end of the game for me."

The band began to play for the half-time show. The dance team lead the band with the flutes section next and then the saxophones. They were to march half way around the track and then meet in the middle facing the opposing team. Amber hated to walk past the cheerleaders because she knew Symphony and Hunter would be the first ones looking at her and judging her. She felt stupid in her band uniform. From the top of her head to the soles of her feet, she didn't feel feminine at all. Amber hated the big hat they had to wear and the strap that had to go across her chin. She felt as if she were wearing a helmet herself. That jacket wasn't any better. If felt huge compared to the skimpy wear the cheerleaders wore. Amber missed a note as she tugged on her tuxedo style pants that were a tad too long. Ugh! This sucks. She thought to herself. Her pants had gotten caught on the heel of her shoes which she thought looked more like ROTC boots.

"I would die if I had to wear a getup like that." Symphony whispered to Hunter while eyeing each band member as they marched passed.

"Oh, you talking to me now?"

"Bitch, you better be glad I am! You already know I don't play that sneaky mess. I don't care if you was my mama."

Symphony gathers all the girls. "It's our turn to go out there. I want to see some pep in y'alls step and smiles on the faces! I bet not see nobody walking." Everyone moaned and groaned because they thought Symphony was a cheer-a-holic. "Hands on ya hips and I want to see heels hitting butts. Ready? Let's go!"

"Davis! I don't know what your problem is, but you better get your butt in gear! The play is not over until you hear the whistle! You know that! How can you just let that man run through you like that?" Coach Thomas clutched the clipboard tightly in his hand as he pointed it in Roman's direction.

Roman knew that he'd let the ball go too early and let the guy go through and score on purpose, but now, he wasn't so sure that was the right thing to do. He felt conflicted. He felt bad for his coach and team if he just threw the game on purpose. He also felt bad if he won and Patrón and Remy made good on their threats to get at Symphony.

It's a few seconds left in the game and the Tigers are on their way to losing the first game of the season. Roman can hear Quincy cheering him on from the sideline, except for all the wrong reasons. His team and coaches are looking defeated. Quincy begs his coach to put him in one last time. Feeling they really had nothing left to lose, he let Quincy in on the last play.

The Cougars kick off the ball and lines it all the way down the field. The ball bounces in front of Quincy Garnett and bounces over him. Even though it's a live ball Quincy ignores it while his teammates are yelling for him to get the ball as they charge full speed towards him. Back by the goal line, Roman Davis is having a fight within himself. Should he or shouldn't he? Roman sees his coach from the sideline cussing and fussing up a frenzy. He grabs the ball and runs to the five, he angles and jump over a few Cougars who have fallen over themselves trying to tackle him. He's up the sideline and still running. He's to the 20… 25… 30… He's to the 40! He's down the sideline and angles left…35…20… He's got blockers! 5… TOUCHDOWN!

Roman has made the winning touchdown! Everyone roars as the team rushes out onto the field to hug Roman, except Quincy. He looks onto the bleachers and sees the twins growling at him and rolling their eyes. He now knows that he has signed a check to the devil and it just bounced.

"Why'd you do that man?" Quincy ran to catch up with Roman.

"'Cause… that's what I do… win."

"Bruh! Remy'em already gave me half the money!"

"Give it back."

To Quincy, Roman just didn't understand the dangers and repercussions that came from dealing with Remy. Walking up to the twins to give them that money back was like taking his final walk to get executed. "Here… give this back to your brother." Quincy said handing the money over to Tanga'Rae.

"Humph! I don't know what you expect for us to do with that?" Tanga'Rae says with her arms still crossed.

"Right! My brother paid you up front for a service that he expected to be delivered. So I suggest you take that up with them." Ta'keyla hissed.

"Just take the damn money!" Quincy stuffed it in Tanga'Rae's folded arms.

"Oh Ta'Keyla… we got some shopping to do, wanna hit up the mall? This fool just gave us a "G"!"

After coming out of the school Symphony ran up to Roman, threw her arms around his neck and kissed him. "I'm so proud of you bae!"

Roman smiles, "For what?"

"For not letting someone dictate to you what you should do. You stood your ground, which shows me you're a real man!"

Roman laughs, "Is that right?"

"Yeah."

"I had to admit. That was the hardest decision ever to make… especially when they had threatened you."

"Huh? What you mean, threatened me?"

"I dunno… Patrón and Remy kept saying stuff like, "If you don't throw the game, we going after ya girl." I kept telling them nigga's that you ain't interested.

"Wait…" Symphony moved a few inches away from Roman. "So… they were threatening to come after me and you think it's to get on with me?"

"Yeah."

"So… it never crossed your mind that they might hurt me?"

"Calm down! Ain't nobody goin' do nothing to you!"

"Oh, and you know this for sure… how?" Symphony was now starting to get upset and it showed. She didn't care who heard or saw. "You know what! Get outta my face… I'm done with you!"

19 CHAPTER NINETEEN
ROMAN DAVIS

You don't accept me for who I am. You judge me, yet you haven't lived in my shoes. If you can't respect me for who I am, leave me alone and let me live my life.

SYMPHONY CAN GET SO dramatic at times. Does she really think I'd let anyone put their hands on her? This whole time she's been the one telling me not to throw the game! She's mad now but she'll get over it.

As soon as we entered into my grandmother's foyer, she lunged and began to chastise Jaylen and me. "Where have y'all been? The game was over hours ago. I've been calling ya cell phone for a while now."

"Oh, my bad, Ma. My battery went out." I threw my jacket on the coat rack beside the front door.

"And what's your excuse?" Ma stopped Jaylen from running upstairs.

"I ain't got no excuse Grandma, I just forgot mines at home."

"What the hell am I paying the bill 'fer then? Y'all obviously don't need 'em."

I wasn't paying Ma' no attention because she often ranted like this. My attention, however; was on the male stranger sitting on my grandmother's sofa. This dude was dressed in an all-black jogging suit that looked like he had to pay a grip for it. He was a dark ass dude with a razor shaved head. On it, it wore an old school Kango which he sported backwards. "Ma, who is that?"

"Well that's what I was trying to tell ya. I told you weeks ago that I needed to talk to ya both, but ya just kept pressin' me off. Both of y'all come on in here." Jaylen and I looked at each other before following Ma into the living room.

"This here, is Mr. Dennis –"She waved her hand as if saying, forget his last name. "It's just Dennis." She introduced Mr. Dennis to Jaylen and me. "Y'all have a seat." She sat down in a chair, Jaylen sat on the other end of the sofa, but I chose to stand.

I didn't trust this dude and not even one word had escaped his mouth. I wasn't about to let my guard down by punking out and having a seat like Jaylen. I'm a soldier. And a soldier has to be ready at all times. Especially when the enemy is invading his camp. Before I even attempted to get comfortable, I had to know what this dudes intentions were.

"I can't believe how you guys have turned into such young men." Dennis rubbed his chin.

"Are we supposed to know who you are or something?" I was defensive and it showed.

"Roman don't be rude! You know that is not the way I've raised you!" Ma readjusted herself in her chair.

Dennis laughed a little and removed his hat to pat the sweat erupting from his baldhead. He was about to open his mouth and say something until Ma beat him to the punch.

"He's your uncle." Evelyn switched to her rocking chair and began to rock. "Yep, you're long lost Uncle Dennis."

"Who's uncle? Not mine!" I know the look on my face said it all. I didn't know this nigga from jump. Never even seen a damn picture of this dude, so don't come up in my space tellin' me jack! On the real!

"He's yours and Jaylen."

"How the hell is that Ma? I know he ain't your son!" My grandmother jumped up and smacked me dead in the mouth. I had to take a deep breath because my reflexes had flinched. I had to catch myself. For a minute, I almost forgot she was my grandmother.

"Not here! Not in my presence will you curse at me boy!"

I had enough of the charades and game playing. I didn't like it at all, almost as much as I didn't like the strange dude sitting in my face. I reached for Ma's purse to get her car keys.

"Roman! What do you think you're doing?" She grabbed her purse away from me and held it close to her breast as if she was about to nurse a newborn baby. "You're going to stop taking my car, you know you don't have a license!"

This made me even more heated. She didn't have a problem with me driving the car when she needed a refill on her prescription or running an errand she didn't want to do. But now. Now, in front of this stranger, she wanted to act as if she set and had reinforce able rules.

"You cannot just drive my car any 'ole time you want too. The next time, I'ma call the law and have them pick you up!"

For me, it all went in one ear and out the other. Dennis the stranger stood up as if he were going to intervene until Ma shut him up and shut him down.

"Come on cuz, let's bounce!" Jaylen got up and followed me.

"I don't care where you go, so as long as it's on foot!" Ma waited for a few moments and then returned to entertain the visitor.

I burst through the screen door letting it bounce back and hit Jaylen in the face. I was too heated to apologize and Jaylen knew not to cross me when I was this upset. I put my hands in my jeans pockets and paced back and forth across the porch.

Jaylen's meek ass just stood still and watched as I vented. "I don't like to be lied to!" I bit my lip so hard I broke the skin and could taste the blood on my tongue. "That's the worst fuckin' thing you could do to me! It's worse than spittin' in my face!" I looked at Jaylen, "You feel me bruh!?" Jaylen remained silent but nodded his head.

Ever since I could remember, I have always had Jaylen's back because he was never able to stand up for himself. Especially when he flunked because the teachers felt he wasn't socially ready to move on so they held him back.

The other kids always made fun of Jaylen because he wasn't as cool and confident as me, but I put a stop to that real quick. I had been into numerous fights and gotten suspended over protecting my cousin. One thing I don't play with is my family.

Since it seemed like we were thrown into the same situation of being born to two different women who didn't give a damn about us, made the two of us develop a rock solid relationship.

"Man, let's walk!" I stepped off all four steps at once.

"Where to?" Jaylen followed behind me like a puppy on a leash.

"See if Q at the crib." No sooner did we reach the corner, rain began to pour down in huge portions. "Fuck!" Me and Jaylen swooped our hoodies onto our heads and began to run back to the house.

"Hop in!" I motioned for Jaylen to get into the passenger's side of Ma's car.

Jaylen thought we were just going to sit inside to get shelter from the rain until I inserted a key and the car came roaring to life. "I thought Grandma wouldn't let you get the key." Jaylen looked nervously at the front door for any signs of Ma.

"She didn't. I been made a copy of the key." I zoom off before Ma could make it outside.

For a while, we just drove around in silence.

"Aw dang!"

"What's the matter?"

"I was supposed to pick of Symph and Q and hit up the movies."

"Oh, it's cool, you can just drop me off at Spirits' if you want."

"If that's what you want. But you know you can roll with us."

"Maybe another time." I knew that Jaylen was going to decline anyway because he and Quincy didn't mesh to well in the first place.

"What do you think is up with that strange Nigga anyway?" I ask Jaylen but all he did was shrug his shoulders as if he didn't know.

I had finally calmed down. I didn't like to let anything or anyone get me out of my hook up. On the rare occasion that it did, I wouldn't stay there too long without working out some kind of plan to get over it.

"How can you just sit over there and be so quiet? Don't nothing get you out your hook -up?" I turn back onto our street heading for Spirit's apartment.

"Not as much as it does you."

"What the hell is that supposed to mean? If it wasn't for me gettin' out my hook-up... nigga they would still be messin' with you."

Jaylen shrugs his shoulders as if saying he didn't care either way.

"I just can't seem to shake that dude; you know what I'm saying?"

Jaylen nods his head in agreement and bite his thumbnail as if he was trying to remove the skin and get to the bone.

"What really pisses me off... is they act like we 'supposed to know this dude! Like we seen him before or some shit. "

Silence.

Jaylen continued to gnaw at his thumb and then he quit... "I have."

I pressed on the breaks so hard it made the back of the car spin into the middle of the street sideways.

20 CHAPTER TWENTY
AMBER STYLES

Instead of a priority, you made me an option. So now you're history, lost and forgotten.

"I CAN'T BELIEVE YOUR mom finally let you spend the night." Willow rummaged through her assortment of DVD's trying to figure out what we should watch for the night.

"I know right." I was a bit nervous and tugged at my pink shirt to make sure it covered half of my butt.

"Why do you keep looking at your watch? You got somewhere to go?" Willow laughed. "Come on, put your pajamas on and let's pop some popcorn and watch one of these Madea movies."

"Dang! I knew I forgot something!" This was my chance to put my plan in motion. "Best friend, I'll be right back. I need to go by my house and grab my pajamas." I grabbed my purse and was ready to bounce. I had told Symphony that I would meet her at her house no later than 9:00pm. It was already 10 after.

"Don't be silly, Amber… you know you can borrow one of mine."

I was at a loss for words. I felt like I was stuck between a rock and a hard place. Never once have I ever done anything like this in my life. I knew I couldn't just come clean and tell Willow the truth, she would never understand anyway. I even thought about just inviting Willow along, but knew she wouldn't go for it. It was as if she thought she was too good for them. Correct that, too good for us.

"I'd feel more comfortable if I had my own." I check my watch again.

Willow looked at me as if I was losing my mind. "You know my parents would have a fit if we went walking this late." Willow folded her arms across her chest and shifted her weight to one foot. "You need to just quit trippin' and grab something of mine."

Willow went into the kitchen to pop some popcorn. I however, went out of Willow's bedroom window. Thank God, there were no roses on the trellis that sat outside her window. I threw my purse down and climbed out backward. The wood on the trellis gave way and broke making my foot slide and loose balance. I was stuck and too far down to go back up. The way I see it, I only had two choices... Yell for help or rip my pants and keep going. I chose to keep going of course. I yank my leg a few times and the wood gave way ripping the seam of my pants. Right now, the only thing that I cared about was getting to my destination. I would have to suffer the consequences, whatever that may be, later. I took off running for Symphony's house because I was already late. I decided to slow down and powerwalk because I was beginning to perspire and didn't bring any extra deodorant.

♥♥♥

"It's about time you got here!" Symphony invited me in. "Hold on and let me call the guys and tell them to come on."

I couldn't believe that I was standing in Symphony's house. Heck, I couldn't believe I just snuck out of Willow's window without even telling her.

Symphony applied my makeup in no time. She even let me borrow some of her accessories and a pair of pants to wear tonight. I couldn't believe how much I loved looking at myself in the mirror now. Just the mere application of makeup covered all my dark spots and had me feeling flawless like the ones I admired.

"I love your hair Symphony."

"Girl, thanks. It's about time for me to get it redone though." Symphony primped some more in the mirror fluffing out her curls one by one. "How come you don't wear none?" Symphony asked me referring to weave.

"I don't know. I want to so bad but my mom won't let me go to the shop."

"Who said you have to go to the shop?" Symphony applied more lipstick and rubbed her lips together after spreading on some gloss. "Your hair ain't that bad. You just need a style. I suggest either cut it shorter or weave it."

"I would love to have my hair like yours." I wanted to touch Symphony's hair so bad to see if it felt as real as it looked but I didn't dare without being invited.

Symphony seemed a bit annoyed. "Ugh... Not like mine. I hate that. Whatever you do, always be you or better than someone else. However, there's no way you can be better than me... but if you get the hair and the glue, I might can do it for you."

I couldn't believe my ears. I felt like a kid in the candy store. Like it was Christmas morning. I ran over to Symphony and threw my arms around her. "OMG!!! Thank you, thank you, thank you!!!"

She removed my arms from around her. "Keep that up and I'm recanting my offer."

"I'm sorry." I try to contain myself from jumping up and down.

"You know what? I'm feeling real generous right now." Symphony began to rummage around her room. "I have a few leftover pieces I can put in your hair right quick."

I wanted to scream but I contained myself as best as I could.

"Stop squirming…"

"I'm sorry, I can't help it… I'm so excited."

"Well, you're going to owe me."

"Whatever it is consider it done!" Symphony glued about four tracks in and flat ironed the ends. I shook my head just to watch the body wiggle and jiggle in the mirror. Oh yeah! I could get use to this!

BEEP! BEEP!

"Finally, they here. Let's go." Symphony grabbed her bag and headed for the door. "Mother! I'm gone!"

"Alright, don't stay out all night Symphony!"

"Wow! You allowed to just leave whenever you want and go out with guys?" I was in awe.

"Girl yes! I'm grown!" Symphony joked. "And what guys? Quincy and Roman ain't nobody!"

My heart was beating a mile a minute when we walked up to the car. I wanted to hurry up and get in the car before Willow started to surveillance the condos looking for me. I was in amazement when I saw Roman driving. He looked like such a man to me sitting in that driver's seat.

Quincy got out of the passenger's seat and let Symphony slide in. I couldn't help the immediate sting of jealousy that instantly plagued my mind. Why couldn't it be me sitting where Symphony now sat.

Trying to accept my fate, I let myself just be happy enough that I was invited in the first place. Quincy told me to slide over behind Roman's seat because my legs were shorter than his were. His seat was pushed back and leaned back even farther.

"What took y'all so long? We goin' be late for the movie." Symphony reached in her purse, pulled out a Newport, and lit it.

I sat in that back seat and thought about how everyone seemed way older than me. I couldn't believe that Roman was driving and Symphony was smoking. I felt like a baby compared to them.

"So what Symp! Either you want to go or you don't! Wassup? "Roman took a long pause at a stop sign awaiting for her response.

Symphony took her time in responding. She was looking out of the window while she inhaled her cigarette. She turned towards Roman, exhaled, and said, "You can waste your money if you want to, but my time is one thing I don't waste."

I wished I could be as cool as Symphony. I studied Symphony as if she was my favorite subject. I admired her self-confidence and the way she dressed. Her white damaged jeans made her legs appear longer. Her yellow heels had to be at least 4-6 inches. Symphony walked in those things as if she was wearing her cheerleading sneakers. I wondered what size shoes Symphony wore because as soon as the opportunity presented itself, I was going to sink my feet into those very shoes and make believe I was her.

"What do you want to do Amber?" Roman slid the gear to park and turned to face me.

I remembered that Roman didn't like me to act shy. Therefore, I tried to plug into Symphony's self-confidence and downloaded some for myself. "It really doesn't matter to me. I'm down with whateva." I grabbed at the scarf that symphony let me borrow to make sure that it was still correctly placed.

Roman laughed. "You hear that Q? She down for whateva."

Symphony looked back at me. "Neva say whateva when you have no idea what's on a nigga's mind." Symphony extended her hand and held her cigarette out toward me. "Hit that, Ms. Whateva."

Seeing that all eyes were on me, I took the cigarette and inhaled. I had the slightest idea of what I was doing and now so did everyone else. I coughed uncontrollably and gagged a few times as if I was going to vomit. "Girl, give me my damn cigarette!" Everyone started laughing. I was so embarrassed that if I were a few shades lighter, you would have seen me turn a bright red.

A car pulled behind us and flashed there brights a few times. After ignoring Roman's hand jesters to go around, Quincy stuck his head out the back window and said, "Go around! Stupid ass!"

The driver finally got the message and pulled around but stopped to shout obscenities and hand out finger jesters to Roman and the rest in the car. I felt uncomfortable and didn't join in. From where I was sitting, I couldn't see the driver but I could see that the passenger was a white woman with Blonde hair.

"If I ever see you again, I'ma blow a hole in that thing you call a face! Little young punk! "

My heart sunk from recognition of the driver's voice but there was no way that it was who I thought it was, especially with the white woman sitting in the front.

Finally, the car had passed and the headlights from Roman's car shined on the license plates. It read, "R. Styles" I sunk so far into my seat you would have sworn I was sitting on the floor of the car.

21 CHAPTER TWENTY-ONE
SYMPHONY PERKINS

I used to want a relationship with no strings attached, but then I realized the strings are what holds a real relationship together.

THIS NIGHT WAS A mess. First of all, Roman comes late, makes me miss the movie, and then everyone just decides to go to the park to turn up and smoke weed. I could sneak and do this at home. On top of all that, Roman had the nerve to act as if he had an attitude when I should still have an attitude from having to watch my back.

"What's wrong with you?" I lit a Newport and blew the smoke into the air.

"What makes you think something is wrong with me?" Roman took a swig of beer. That was the strongest thing we could cop. "Stop acting like you know me."

"We been kickin' it for how long now?" I grabbed the beer from Roman's hand and gulped it.

"Man, you need to stop acting like you care!"

It took all the strength in me to not react negatively towards Roman's attitude, obviously, something was bothering him big time. It could be the fact that he won the game knowing that them weed heads are probably going to be up to something. I took a deep breath, held my head all the way back and gazed at the night stars.

"What's really going on Roman? You know you can talk to me, just like I know I can come to you for anything." I kicked off my heels and got down on my knees so I could be face to face with Roman who was sitting on a rail. I felt bad knowing that all this time I was the one telling him to be his own man and not throw the game.

"Yeah, you must be serious if you're going to kneel on this dirty damp ground in your white jeans." Roman and I laughed for a brief minute.

"I don't care about no stupid clothes. All this stuff is superficial. It certainly don't mean more to me than you." I looked him in his eyes and smiled. "I'm sorry for going off on you earlier."

"I know babe. It's all good."

Roman grabbed me by the hands to help lift me from the ground. "Thanks because although I don't care about these jeans… that ground was killing my knees."

"Want to take a walk around the park?"

"Sure, what about them?" We both looked back at Quincy and Amber who were sitting on the swings passing a joint back and forth.

"Looks like a match made in Heaven."

"Yeah right! Hunter ain't going to be having that." I thought about her funky attitude. "Oh well, if she wanted her man she should have come." I be dammed if I be a boyfriend babysitter.

We walked circles around the park talking and sharing our thoughts but Roman didn't dare tell me what he was really mad about. I didn't know what he was hiding or keeping from me.

"Since when did you start drinking anyway?" I stopped and sat on a nearby bench. My feet were starting to hurt and there was no way I was going to walk barefoot in that damp grass, not knowing what was in it.

"I just took a sip." Roman shrugged his shoulders and sat beside me. "I was mostly just holding it until you took it from me. Why do you smoke so much?"

I was about to light another Newport until Roman said that. "I don't smoke so much. It just helps calm my nerves I guess, gives me something to do."

"You still having those dreams?"

"Dreams? I wish. More like nightmares."

"You want to talk about it?"

"No. Not really… not right now, anyways." I lit the Newport.

"I feel you."

I place my feet in Roman's lap and he began to massage them. "What do you think is up with Hunter? Ever since she got back she been acting bugged out."

"I don't know. Maybe she got too much on her."

"Like what? Babysitting her bratty brothers? We all had to do that at some point in time." I blew smoke into the air. "I have to watch my sister sometimes but that still doesn't hinder me and my plans."

"True. But then again, it's just you and your sister. She has to play mama to… what… three? Four brothers?"

"I know. But it wasn't always like that. It's like she changed after she went to stay with her grandmother and being homeschooled there." I took a few more puffs and flicked my cigarette butt onto the sidewalk.

"Who knows? Maybe she still dealing with the loss of her grandmother." Roman stopped rubbing my feet and cracked his knuckles. "You never really know how or how long people mourn. Ya know?"

"True. Sometimes I just wish I had my girl back." I grabbed my cell phone to check the time. "Dang! It's after midnight."

"Man, I guess I better get my grandmother's car back before she starts trippin'."

Roman and I were cleaning out the car trying to spray away and signs of wrongdoing. "Y'all better come on because I will leave y'all right here!" Roman yells to Amber and Quincy.

"We coming!" Quincy empties the rest of the beer into his mouth, crushes the can, and misses the trash can by two inches.

"Dude! You serious? Pick it up." Quincy waves Roman off with his hands and continues to kiss on Amber.

"Who is you? The park ranger?" I could tell that Roman was annoyed. He picks the can up and throws it in the trash himself. "That's what I thought, nigga."

I snatch Amber away from Quincy to talk with her in private. "You do know that you all up on Hunter's man, right?"

Amber's eyes were squinted like it took all the energy she had to keep them open. "That ain't what he told me."

"I don't give a damn what he told you! A nigga will lie about anything to get into your drawers."

"Whateva! He cool peoples." Amber reaches into her pockets and pulls out a half smoked joint. "You want to hit this?"

I smack her hand away. "No! And you shouldn't either!"

Amber looks at me as if I was trying to play a goody-2-shoes role. "You be sleepin' with niggas, smokin' cigarettes, and drinkin' and you trying to tell me you don't smoke weed?"

"First of all, little girl! You don't know me to say I sleep with niggas! You don't know shit about me or what I do! Now, I know you high and all right now, so I'ma let that go! Get in the car!"

Roman already had the car running and sitting in the car ready to go. Before the rest of us could get in, we saw flashing red lights and heard a WHOOP! WHOOP!

22 CHAPTER TWENTY-TWO
AMBER STYLES

Sometime I feel like an empty bottle with a hole on the bottom. No matter how many times I try to fill it, it just becomes empty again.

I COULD HAVE PEED my pants. I had never in my life been in a situation like this, let alone see a real life cop close up. Roman stepped out the car awaiting the officer to approach him while Symphony, Quincy, and me were on the passenger side of the car. The officer held his had up to tell us to stay where we were.

"Can I see your license, registration, and proof of insurance please?" It was more of a demand than a question.

"Uh..." Roman looked at Symphony and Symphony used her hands, head, and eyes to say she didn't know what to do. "The registration should be in the glove compartment." The officer allowed Roman to reach over to the passenger's side to retrieve it.

"Who is Evelyn Haynes?"

"Th-that's my grandmother... sir."

My legs were shaking so bad I thought I was going to fall to the ground. I was scared out of my mind. I began praying to God. "Oh Lord, Jesus! If you get me out of this, I promise I will never sneak out the house again."

"Oh! That's nice... you're praying for yourself. What about the rest of us, you selfish chick!" Symphony whispered in my ear.

"I'm sorry! But I'm scared!" I looked at Symphony with tears in my eyes. "I ain't never been in a situation like this before!"

"Oh, and we have? Quit thinking you're that high and mighty bitch!" Symphony rolled her eyes at me. I looked over at Quincy with his hands in his pockets fidgeting around like he was nervous.

"Stop calling me that! I don't know what to do!" The tears that swelled up in my eyes had rolled down my cheeks.

Quincy had taken his hands out of his pockets and grabbed my hand and held it. I looked up at him quizzically. "Put it in your pocket and run!" I didn't think twice. I placed the baggy in my pocket and took off running like I was a track star. I didn't stop to look back. In my mind, the police stopped interrogating Roman and took off to run after me.

My first thought was to run back to Willow's house. But then I thought bad mistake. That chick probably mad as hell at me right now. I'll just have to go home and think of some excuse to tell my mom when that time comes. After I give Willow a little time to cool off from sneaking out on her, I'm sure she'll understand and forgive me as usual. Either way it go, even if she mad, she'll have my back. When I get in the house, I'll just let her phone ring once. That's our code for if you hear it, call me back… she'll know it's me. She might not call back tonight though. I'm sure she salty.

All the way home I kept looking around every corner wondering if the cops were going to swoop in on me. I kept envisioning them finding me, searching me, finding this weed, handcuffing me, and taking me to jail. I took the baggie out of my pocket and my first thought was to throw it somewhere as I was running. But then I thought, couldn't they find my fingerprint on the bag? Or my DNA from the half smoked one? I put them back in my pocket and kept it moving.

My first thought when Quincy handed me that stuff and told me to run. I thought I was doing them a solid by taking the chance and running with his stash. Even though I was scared, I felt like a real ride or die chick after I got out of their eyesight. Then I wondered about Symphony. Did she count me as faithful doing this? Or to her, does it look like I was abandoning them? OMG… my head was spinning trying to figure all this stuff out. It just seemed like everyone in the world was gonna hate me. But then again, I do think too much. I over think things. And half the time, the things I think about happening, don't even be as half bad as I thought in the first place. Ok, new thought… Willow got my back and she will definitely cover for me. My mom will never find out about this. And the squad will have to love me for what I did. Yep, that's it.

It felt weird putting my house key in the door at almost 3:00 in the morning. I tried to mask my fear with the thought of me being grown and this was my house. What do ya know. I'm home. I'm safe. No cops. No arrest. No parents. I'm good. I got away with it. I open the front door and walk in.

SMACK! I fall to the floor taking the tableside lamp with me. What the hell! Am I being robbed? Am I about to be killed for walking in on the robbers?

"Get yo ass up!"

Oh hecks naw! That wasn't no robber. That was my mom! She grabs my 90-pound frame up as if it were a bag of feathers and throw me into the wall. "Where the hell were you?"

I didn't know what to say. I didn't say anything. I think I was in shock. I just look at her and stare. The phone rings again and she picks it up and answers. "What? Yeah she's here! Her little ass just came walking up in here a few minutes ago." She hangs the phone up and gets back in my face. "Do you know we were all worried about you? When Kathy called me at work and said you were gone and how they came to the house looking for you and yo ass wasn't here!" So Willow did snitch on me. She didn't have my back at all! "I want to know where the hell you were!"

"Out!" That was the only word that came out of my mouth. I didn't know what to say. I hadn't thought about it. I'd never even considered myself being in this situation. I didn't want to tell her who I was really with because then I'd be a snitch just like Willow.

She smacks me again in my face. This time twice. Three times. Then it just became a smack fest. I throw my arms up to protect my face and shield her hits which became punches in my head until my dad busts through the door and pulls her off of me. "What is this mess you have in your hair?" My mom starts rummaging through the tracks Symphony had glued in and began to rip them out. "Take yo ass in the room and get ready." She snatches the belt from around my father's waist so quick and smooth you wouldn't even have thought it was buckled.

"You can't whoop me!" O my Lord, I don't know what was coming over me. It was like it wasn't even me.

"I can't whoop you? O, I see. You think you're too big for an ass whoopin' huh?" She throws the belt to the floor and gets in a stance with her fist up. "You think you're a woman now? You think you can go toe-to-toe with me? You think you can whoop my ass? Girl I will beat you like a bitch in the street!" Before she had a chance to swing on me my dad takes hold of her and tells her to calm down. I have never in my life seen my mom go off like that. She looked straight up like a ghetto hood rat.

"You better get her!" My mom walks away from us and go into the kitchen to light a cigarette.

"When did you start back smoking?" My dad asks my mom. I never even knew she ever smoked.

"When this bitch right here decided she was grown enough to sneak the fuck out. That's when." She took long big puffs… not small dainty ones like Symphony.

"Come on… give me that." My dad tries to take the cigarette from my mom but she gives him an evil look that could have blew up the whole house. He wasn't stupid. He knew when to back off and leave my mother alone.

He leaves my mother in the kitchen and comes to talk to me. "What's going on sweetheart?"

"Nothing. She tripping." I fold my arms across my chest and they heave up and down in rhythm to my breathing.

"Something is going on. Where were you?" I wanted to ask him the same thing. Where were you? I wanted to say, I saw you in the car with some white woman and spewing out obscenities to young kids. But I didn't. I just thought it.

I still didn't come up with an answer. Tears continued to stream down my face like a leaky faucet. I wasn't like boo-hoo crying or nothing. It's just that I couldn't control my tears because I was so mad. "Daddy, I was just out with my friends. We went to the movies. That's all. Honest. But mommy don't understand that." I literally smack my cheek and wipe my hand firmly across it to remove the tear stains.

"Well. Your mother's just looking out for your best interest. You know that."

"But she don't let me go anywhere or do anything! It's like I'm a prisoner in here. Like I'm locked up and she won't let me out." The old Akon lyrics popped into my head. "I want to come stay with you daddy."

He began to laugh like something was funny. "You just mad right now." He rubs the hair on his chin. "This will all blow over in a little while." Humph… what a lame ass answer. Technically he didn't even give me one. He laughed at me like I was a damn joke. He not about to get out of this so easily.

"Why can't I stay with you, daddy?" I beg my own father to take me in.

"You want to go live with this sorry ass man? Go right the hell ahead!" She mushes me as she walks pass and go into my room to gather all my clothes. She begins tossing them at me. At my dad. And outside. "Get the hell out!" I mean really! She was blowing everything all out of proportion. The phone rings again. "Hello!" She snatches up the receiver and yells into it. I guess the caller didn't say anything because she hangs up even more furious. "You need to tell ya little damn friends to stop calling my house and not saying shit!"

Little friends? I thought to myself. At first when the phone was ringing, I thought maybe it was Willow doing our code thing. But she wouldn't do it more than once, especially knowing that I'm in full blown trouble mode at this moment. Could it have been Symphony? Roman? Or maybe even Quincy? Yeah it may have been Quincy wondering about his stash.

My dad was picking up all my clothes and bringing them back into the house. "Stop acting so dramatic Joi! You know she can't come stay with me!"

Boom there it was! He couldn't tell me but he could tell my mom flat out. He didn't want me to stay with him. I see he tried to at first blame it on my mom like she wouldn't let me. But what was his excuse now? She was practically throwing me out and he still wouldn't take me.

"Why the hell not Russell?"

"I ain't got no place for a kid! You know that Joi!"

"Well according to her… she's not a kid anymore!"

"I can't do it… and I'm not going to do it!" I felt like an invisible misfit. Both of my parents were fighting over me. But not in a good way. They were fighting because neither of them wanted me. I run to my room and for the first time that I could remember, I slam my door closed and lock it.

♥♥♥

I could hear my mom's boyfriend, Keith, coming in as my father was going out. I hear my mom's voice change too. It wasn't as violent as it was when she was talking to my dad. Now she sounded fake and phony. I mimic her with my facial expressions on how her face and gestures would be when she's talking to Keith. So fake. Now she wants to act like a drama queen. Like she's so distraught. Give me a break!

I sit there on the floor at the bottom of my bed holding my knees in my arms. I replayed back all the events that had taken place today. This day was bananas! I reminisced about when Quincy had kissed me. Any other time, in a situation like that, I would have been scared to death. Shoot… when he kissed me, I closed my eyes and imagined I was kissing Roman. I ain't never smoked weed before… but I think I like it. It was like it gave me confidence and made it real easy to do the things I thought about doing before over thinking it.

My mom's boyfriend knocks on my door pulling me out of my thoughts. "I'm about to take your mom for a little ride so she can cool off. You going to be alright?"

Hump! As if he really gave a damn. I didn't even answer. He knocks on the door a few more times and then walks away. I could hear his car start up and pull off. I was glad they were gone. I sit there for a few minutes feeling sorry for myself. I reach into my pocket and pull out the half-smoked joint. Realizing I didn't have a lighter, I run into the kitchen to light it on the stove and then run back and lock my bedroom door and began to puff and blow the smoke out the window. I could hear the birds beginning to chirp. It just dawned on me that I haven't even been to sleep yet.

♥♥♥

My mom comes waking me up early in the morning. I feels like I had just closed my eyes. I look at the clock on my nightstand. I did just close my eyes! She must be crazy thinking I'm going to church today with all that went down last night.

"Hurry up and get dressed. I might just have Pastor lay his hands on you today." What kind of comment was that! Maybe Pastor needs to lay his hands on her because if I'm not mistaken, she just walked in the house. And last time I checked… she was NOT out with her husband.

I take a quick shower and get dressed. I wasn't even feeling all that getting dressed up in your Sunday's best. I threw on me a pair of jeans, a button up top, and some sneakers. My mother comes into my room. "Oh, is it Youth Sunday?"

"No."

"Then why the disrespect."

"What?" I didn't understand what she was talking about.

"Stop with the "what's" Amber. Enough of all that. Put on something that makes it look like you're going to church."

"I don't have nothing else. You threw all of my stuff on the floor and out the door, remember?"

"Oh." My mom leaves out of the room and comes back with a small box in her hand. She sits on the edge of my bed and puts her hand on my knee. "Look Amber, I get it. I really do. But you cannot… you will not, be disrespectful to me or anyone for that matter. Now, I apologize for my part last night. I'm not sorry I went off on you! Don't get it twisted. I'm apologizing because I know I could have handled it in a better manner than I did. Do you understand?"

I nod my head yeah. She stands and waits for me to say something. I'm guessing she wants me to apologize too. I don't see why I have to. The only thing I was sorry about was getting caught. I was sorry I had a snitchin' ass friend. But she still eyeballing me. Fine! "I'm sorry to for sneaking out, mom."

"Promise you won't do it again?"

"Yeah, I promise." Whatever. This ain't no genuine apology or promise. It's like she's actually making me say these things. Sure I promise I won't sneak out again. Probably until I do again! I don't even know what's going to be happening later on today! Whatever!

She hands me the box she'd been holding in her hand. "I know it's not much… but it's all I can do right now."

I was getting a little excited! We don't normally exchange gifts unless it's Christmas. I opened the box and my eyes were bugged out! I couldn't believe she got me a cell phone! AHHHHHH!

And then the smile and the happiness fades away as quick as it had first come. Really! Really! This was like an ungift, if that was even a word. Really! An Obama phone! Who am I? Grandma! I look the phone over, trying to keep of the façade as best I could but I don't think it was working. It was like she lifted me up just to throw me back down into a pile of dog poop. No worse… elephant poop.

"What's wrong?" My mom's smile now fades too.

"Nothing." I look up at her and force a smile. "Thanks mom."

"Well geesh Amber. Don't act too thrilled. I know it's not one of those expensive phones but give me a break!"

What did she want me to do? Jump up and down and act as fake as she was when Keith showed up last night? I'm sorry. I'm just not that great of an actress. "No mom, it's cool. I like it. Thanks." If anybody saw this ugly cheap stupid phone, I'd really be a laughing stock at Westbrook High. She talking about all these bills she gotta pay. She not even paying for this stupid phone. It's Free! And it's not like I can even talk on it. 250 monthly minutes! Really! That's like an emergency only phone! Oh… I get it now. It for just in case I try to pull a disappearing act, she can call me. Ha! Well little do she know, that won't work if I don't answer? Or have minutes left. Now see, if she had got a smartphone, she might could have tracked me.

♥♥♥

It was offering time at the Deliverance Center and today we had a guess pastor by the name of Pastor Andrews from Life Church Ministries. He was a dark skinned man who didn't look as if he'd miss too many meals. But I could tell that his only taste wasn't just in food. His 3-piece suit was all that and a bag of chips. He was so huge though that his suits had to be tailor-made. Each of his finger held mounds of gold and diamonds just like the watch on his wrist. He didn't waste any time in showing them off. His many blessings as he called it. Says that if we would be faithful tithers, we could get some of that stuff too.

It was time for our row of pews to be ushered out next. My mom grabs my granny's tithing envelope to put in the offering because she couldn't get around as good as she used to. No sooner than everyone sat back down and get comfortable in the pews, Pastor Andrews starts again.

"Will a man rob God?" The portly man holds onto the podium as he spoke to his borrowed members.

I watch as my mother folds her arms and rolls her eyes toward the cathedral ceilings. "Here we go."

Granny slaps my mom on her knee. "You stop that in God's house ya here!"

It was funny to see my own mom get chastised by her mother. Maybe it was true what they say. No matter how old you are, you're never grown to your own parents.

"Come on Saints!" Pastor Andrews roared as he wipes his dripping forehead with a towel. "I know you can do better than that! Now, I want y'all to reaaaachhh way down and give a better offering than that to the Lord! Ain't He been good to ya!"

The congregation cries Amen in unison including Granny. "Now I don't want anyone to give less than $100!"

"He crazy as hell!" I know my mom didn't mean to take it that far but it slipped out and it was too late to take it back. Now maybe she'll know how I feel sometimes.

I cover my mouth with my hands and giggle like a grade-schooler. I look at Cam'Ron and he can care less. He's using the old elbow on the knee to use his hand as a kickstand for his face. I bend down to try and see his face more clearly. Yup, he's sleep. I look further down my pew to see if Ryder or Willow heard my mom. They did, Ryder smiles a little but Willow mean mugs me as if my mother was my child and for me to get a handle on her. Ugh! Still not talking to her right now so she can just turn her snitchin' eyes elsewhere.

"Don't you blaspheme in God's house! You need to run up to the alter and repent!" Granny was embarrassed that her own daughter would say such a thing as that. She knew she had raised her better. I know granny was thanking God no one else had heard my mom's nonsense. Granny grabs her pocketbook to get her last $100 she had to her name for the rest of the month.

"Mama! What are you doing?" I hear my mom whisper to granny as she snatches her purse from her.

"I'm listening to the man of God you 'ole blasphemer!"

"Well, I'm a child of God and you are not about to give no more money to this man! He ain't even our Pastor."

"How do you think I get all the money I have to help you out all the time? By being obedient, that's how. Granny tried her best to scoot away from my mother. "What are you doing now?"

"I am getting away from you, 'cause I know the good Lord bout to strike you down and I don't want to be nowhere near."

23 CHAPTER TWENTY-THREE
ROMAN DAVIS

In all honesty I think that I'm afraid of being happy. Because whenever I get too happy, something bad always happens.

I DIDN'T APPRECIATE THE little scared straight joke Ma had played on me. Yeah I took her car without asking but so what, it wasn't like it was the first time. I admit, at first I was scared shitless.

"Damn man, why the hell didn't you make a spare key of the spare key?"

"Quincy, shut the hell up and keep looking!" By the time we find out where Ma hid the key she'd be back. I searched all of her hiding spots and still haven't been able to locate it yet. In a minute, I'm just going to give up and say she must have it on her.

"Did y'all ever find out who that dude was?"

"Who told you about that?"

"Jaylen, told me."

"Since when did you and Jaylen become so cool that y'all started sharing heart to hearts?" I continue to search through my grandmother's drawers and little trinkets and knick-knacks on top of it.

"Don't get it twisted nigga, it fo damn sho wasn't no heart to heart." Quincy began to search through Ma's overstuffed closet. "You should have seen yo face when that cop pulled up!" Quincy began to laugh at my expense.

"Nigga please! You know yo ass was scared too!"

"Yeah, scared 'cause I had that shit on me.... Did you see how fast Amber high-tailed it out of there?" I couldn't help but join in laughing. "She was running so hard she was kickin' her own ass all the way!"

"I can't believe you gave her yo stash in a situation like that, man that was fowl… even for you." I got serious for a moment thinking of the ramifications that could have really transpired from that.

"I can't believe Ma had a cop friend of hers find you to teach you a lesson."

"Thank God it was fake though."

"Damn!" Quincy had tilted over a box that sat high up inside of Ma's closet. It all came crashing down on his head and buried his Jordans.

I looked over at him, "Dude, really? You better pick all that up and put it right back like she had it." I shake my head and keep my search going on my side of the room.

"You know Remy and Patrón ain't letting that go so easily right?"

"Didn't you give them the money back?" I look up at Q who wore a weird look on his face. "You didn't give it back?"

"Yeah I gave it back!" Quincy began stuffing the things back into the box. "Thing is… I gave it to the twins to give back to 'em… now he say, I ain't give him nothing. Said, whatever I gave to the twins, I gave to the twins!" He emphasized pointing to himself with his thumb. "So, he saying we still owe him a grand or he coming after us!"

"How he goin' be coming after us when I haven't made no agreement with them or touch any of that money?"

"What the hell!" I look over at Q being nosey and reading what appeared to be stacks of mail.

"Can you ever mind yo own business bruh? Just put it back and hurry up!"

"Quincy!" He continued to ignore me and just kept reading. I jump across Ma's bed and snatch the letters from his hand and start placing them back in the box.

"Don't you want to read 'em first?"

"No! I don't!" I grab handfuls of the piles and began raking them back into the box. Quincy grabs my wrist to stop me.

"Read… the… damn… letters man!"

Since he was taking it so seriously, I pause for a moment and began to read the envelopes. "Evelyn Haynes… Evenly Haynes… Evelyn Haynes….." I look up at Q and shrug my shoulders, "So what? They all address to Ma."

"You can't be that fuckin' naive! Up here! Up here!" He began to point to the upper left hand corner.

I seen it. But I don't think I wanted to see it. Or maybe I just didn't want to see it in front of Q. I-I-I don't know. I do know… I'm not dealing with this right now… now is not the time. I start piling all the stuff back into the box.

"What is you doing man? Don't you want to know?"

"Hell no! I ain't been knowing! What the hell is knowing going to do now? W-W-What is it going to change?" I began to stutter. "Shit!" I cram the box of secrets that my grandmother had obviously been hiding from me back onto the shelf.

"Man, you ain't going to at least—"

"No!" I didn't want to talk about it. I didn't want to deal with it and I didn't want company anymore either.

"What about my demo? I need to turn that in ASAP… tomorrow the last day but I wanted to at least get it in today."

"Bounce nigga!" I usher Q to the front door. "No disrespect." I tried to calm myself down because I know Q was only trying to be a friend but right now I didn't need no damn friend. "I know your trying to look out for a brother—"

"I get it Ro… ain't no thang man…hit me up when you can. Please don't forget that demo bruh… I'm a need that within the hour."

"I got you! Within the hour. Keep this on the low… about the letters, nobody but you and me… you got that bruh?"

"Yeah… I got it…within the hour tho."

♥♥♥

I never told Quincy about Remy and Patrón hounding me for a CD. That dude gets extremely out of his hook-up on petty thangs. I burned Q's demo and I just picked some random beat for Patrón and Remy. I got them both with me just in case I run into them fools on my way to Q's. Maybe they'll just take this stupid beat and go on about their business.

Before I can even reach Q's house, these fools pull up right alongside me. "You know, you's a lil dumb nigga. I asked you to do one simple thing." Remy stops and looks at Patrón. "Scratch that… two things."

"I-I-I got your CD right here."

"Oh! You hear that 'P' he finally got the CD weeks later. That must be a badass beat since it took you so long! Hand it here."

I fumble with the CD and hand Remy the one I intended for him to have. "We square right?" I continue to head on to Q's house.

"Holdup!" Patrón gets out of the passenger's side and hold on to my shoulder as Remy pop the CD into his car stereo.

"So, you've been working on this beat for weeks, huh?" Remy turns and looks at Patrón instead of me. "What you think, 'P' does it sound like he worked really hard on this here?" Patrón shakes his head no. "I don't think so either. Lemme see the other CD?"

"What other CD?"

"The other CD in your pocket nigga!" Patrón snatches Quincy's demo from my pocket and hands it to Remy. "Dayum! Now that beat is fire right there!"

"NO! That CD is for a paying customer."

"Paying customer? I think I'm a bit hurt at that comment. I believe we already paid you a grand that you didn't deliver on. I'm pretty sure that trumps whatever this chump paid you for this beat."

"What! No… Q gave you that grand back!" I try to dive in the car over Remy to reach his CD player. They both laugh at me and push me back.

"You sure you want to attempt that again, bruh?" Remy slightly lifts his shirt to expose the gun he wore on his hip. I take a few steps back and raise my hands to surrender. All he needed to do in order for me to let them have the CD was show me that gun. Was the beat that serious to them? Did it mean that much? I wasn't trying to get shot up for nobody's demo. I can't lie, I was more scared now than when the cops pulled up on us last night. After they pull off, I stand there for a minute because I wasn't 100% sure my legs were working yet. I walk a little bit and then run back to the house to burn Quincy another demo of his to turn in for the contest.

I turn my computer back on and a blue screen comes up. I restart it three more times and each time I get the same result. Quincy has already called and texted and I told him both times that I was on my way. I didn't tell him about the run in with Remy and Patrón because I didn't want to hear his mouth.

"Jaylen! You know what's up with this?" I show him what the computer is doing.

"Naw… I ain't never seen that before."

I try wracking my brain to hurry up and figure this thing out but I keep coming up empty.

"Ryder might know tho… I hear he good at computers."

"Sweet! Call him."

"I won't be able to get in touch with him until tomorrow when we at school."

"Fine. Or maybe we can catch him at his bus stop in the morning and see wassup?" I know Q was going to be heated but it was nothing I could do right now. Besides its already late and it's not like he can turn it in now anyway.

Jaylen and I leave the house a few minutes earlier so we could catch Ryder before we got on the bus. But of course who was standing there when we leave out the door, nobody but Quincy wanting to know what was up and why I was ignoring his call.

We hightail it to Ryder's bus stop and when we get up to him, he jumps. "Ryder, can we holla at you right quick?" I tell him what's going on with the computer.

"I-I-I don't r-really know unless I s-s-see it."

"Cool! Let's roll now then!" Q jumps in interrupting.

"Bruh, calm down… I gotta test today… we can handle it when we get home. You down, Ryder?" I asked him because he was standing there looking lost. We start walking back to his bus stop.

"Y-Yeah… I'm d-d-down."

♥♥♥

After school, the four of us dash off the bus and run all the way to my house. I feel bad because I do know how important this contest is to Q. If I didn't have that test today, I might would have flicked to get it done seeing how this is all my fault anyway.

"Y-You have a v-virus."

"Virus? Okay so what do we have to do to get it running again?"

"Only t-t-thing to really d-d-do…is r-reinstall a f-fresh copy of w-w-windows. D-Do you have a r-restore CD?"

"No."

"So, my demo, the beat… it's just gone?" Quincy wanted to know.

"My software? Everything?"

"Man, forget your software!"

"My software is what made your demo!" I turn to Ryder. "What can we do now then?"

"I-I have a windows CD at h-h-home. D-Did you ever b-b-back up your s-s-stuff on a h-hard drive?"

"Nah."

"Ah come on! This is a waste of time. I might as well just forget it!"

I tell Q, "Calm down man and stop being so negative."

While Ryder reinstalls a fresh copy of windows on my computer I remember that I did burn the beat on a CD. The only thing was, we had to sift through all the CD's in my room. Some looked through the mounds of CDs on my many spindles and I sifted through the ones that were sprawled out on the floor.

Having nothing else to loose but time, I re-downloaded the software I used to make Quincy's demo. Found the beat on CD and began to record Quincy as he rapped his song, "Son of a Battlefield." He was flowing nicely but kept messing up and having to restart from the beginning each time.

"Damn! This is useless! I'm not going to make it!"

"Q! Calm down and do it right! If you keep trying to rush through the song… we won't make it! We got a little less than two hours to get there."

He calms down and we make it through for the last time. I snatch the CD from the burner and toss it on the floor with the rest of the cluttered collection and burn a fresh demo.

"How we goin' get it there in less than an hour?" Quincy paste back and forth.

"Roman… I needs you to go grab my prescriptions from the pharmacy and put some gas in the car first."

"Ma! I'm busy right now!" Q stops in his steps and bugs his eyes at me letting me know this was our way to get the demo to the station. "Alright Ma, give me the keys and stuff."

"Don't go nowhere else, Roman. And don't you ever make another copy of my keys again, ya hear me?"

"Yes, Ma." Soon as Ma tosses me the keys and gas money, the CD ejects itself. I snatch it from the base and hand it to Q as if handing him a baton in a relay race. We all follow suit and run from the room.

CRACK! Jaylen steps on one of the CDs and cracks it to pieces. "Come on!" I yell at him. "Don't worry about that right now… we have to go!"

I turn the blinker on to turn into the gas station. "What are you doing?"

"Ma said to get gas first."

Quincy leans over to check the gauge. "Naw… we got enough to get there… just keep going."

I shrug it off and continue on to the radio station.

"I just want to give everybody they props and not letting me give up." Quincy smiles to himself and swallows before continuing on. "Ro, for doing all this for me. Jaylen, for thinking about Ryder. And Ryder, for coming to the rescue." He turns to look in the backseat. "Really man, you don't even hang with us… but you came through and did the impossible." He gives Ryder dap.

"Alright… alright… cut all the sappiness before you start balling into tears." Everyone starts laughing. But we felt the heartfelt of Q's words and it made me feel good to go above and beyond to get his demo to the station.

The car began to slow down and hesitate until it rolls to a complete stop.

"What's going on?" Quincy asked.

I try to turn the ignition again. Nothing. I look at Quincy. "I think we out of gas."

"You have gots to be kidding me!" Quincy raises his hand and pounds himself in the head.

"I-Isn't the s-station a couple of b-blocks that-a-way?"

Without saying another word to each other, I put the car in neutral and the guys began to push it to safety. Q grabs the CD from the car, I lock the doors, and we all take off running in the direction of the radio station.

"Don't even bother. They not taking nomore people." A broke down wannabe Nicki Minaj spat in our direction.

"What?" I look at my cell to check the time; it was just a few minutes after six.

"Man, forget that! I'm going in… we done went through too much to just say forget it off of what one person says." Quincy rushes in through the door and we all follow suit.

Quincy heads up to the front desk and without even looking up, the receptionist speaks before Quincy can get a word in edgewise. "We not takin' no more demos, the contest is closed." She continues to ignore Q and goes back to speaking into her headset.

"That's bullshit!" Quincy begins to cause a ruckus. He looks at the clock on the wall. "It's not even five minutes after! Naw, I want to see the manager!"

We gather around Q to try to calm him down and let him know that acting like that is not the way to get things done. I go back to the front desk and asked the receptionist if we could please speak to the person that's head of the contest.

"Do you have an appointment?" I look at her like she was stupid because she knew I didn't have an appointment.

"Can we please just speak to the person in charge? It's an emergency." I tried my best to speak for Q.

She presses a button and says, "DW, there's some kids here that's dying to see you." She looks up at me and rolls her eyes. "Have a seat."

After waiting fifteen minutes we were getting antsy thinking that this DW character wasn't going to show after all. A few men walk out moments later, sporting tailor-made suits so I know they had to be of importance. On the finger of one man, held a huge gold ring with the initials iced out in bling that read, DW.

"That's him right there!" I shrug Quincy. "Black suit, red tie… go!"

Quincy walks up to the men and breaks in to the conversation politely. He explains his situation and the guy completely ignores anything he said.

"Point blank. The contest closed at 6:00. Not 6:01. Not 6:02. And definitely not 6:45. I'm sorry son but rules are rules and we at Gimmie Sum DAP Records pride ourselves on the straight and narrow. We don't cheat our artist or ourselves." The men in back of him began to giggle like little school girls.

"You're from DAP Records… not the radio station?"

"Yes. I was here to supervise the entries for the contest to make sure that there's no funny business going on…like allowing someone to enter past the allotted time."

"Okay, well forget the contest. Can you just take my demo and listen to it?" I could tell that Quincy was getting beside himself because he was getting nowhere with this DW character. Quincy was losing all sight of himself. Putting himself out there and doing something that he never would have ever done otherwise. Beg.

"Humph!" DW puts his hand in Q's face and wave it. "No solicitation." He and the other guys he was with left out the door leaving Quincy to pick up his pride and any self-respect he had left off the floor.

Quincy stood there for a while in that same spot where those men left him. We stayed seated in the lobby chairs and waited, not taking our eyes off of Q. When he finally turned to leave out the door, so did we.

Quincy stopped at the edge of the parking lot, broke his demo in half, and kicked it in the gutter. "I hate this freakin' life! With the shit I got going for me, I'll never be nothing! I might as well be dead!" Q takes off walking down the street.

Ryder catches up to him and says, "Y-y-you never know what God has in s-s-tore for you. It c-c-could be a r-reason why God d-didn't want you to g-g-go through those d-d-doors."

"Shut the hell up talking to me gay boy!"

"I-I'm not g-gay! I'm j-just saying that s-s-sometimes we might not r-realize why God won't let us do s-s-something no m-m-matter how hard we t-t-try. You might f-find out later on d-down the line."

We all knew that when Q got out his hook-up to just leave him alone until he cooled off. But Ryder didn't know that because he never hung with us.

Q gets up in Ryder's face. "Why the hell do you keep talkin' to me nigga! Ain't neva had a bitch since a bitch had you! You don't know what the hell I'm dealing with or what I'm going through!" Q was so heated. It was the first time we had seen anything that resembled a tear fall from is eye. "Somebody betta' get this faggot ass nigga before I drop his ass!"

Quincy stops and sits on the curb and began to ball his eyes out. No one has ever seen any of us cry. I didn't even think it was possible, let alone think I'd ever see Q of all people doing it. He was ballin' so bad I think tears began to swell up in all of our eyes. I took my eyes off him because I'd be damn if I be the next nigga in line to drop some tears for another nigga.

I tell you what though. Seeing Q sitting there crying, almost made me wish I'd taken that bullet that Remy was willing to exchange for Quincy's demo. But in all honesty, if he'd shot me, he just take the demo anyway. I knew Q was passionate about his music, but I didn't realize the extent of it. I thought he didn't really care that much about anything, but obviously music, was his life, the way football was mine.

Jaylen and I got to Ryder just before he touches Q's shoulder and stroll him a few feet away from Q. "I-I just want him t-t-to know that we're h-here and we u-understand."

I tell Ryder, "Just give him a minute and let him have his space. He knows we're here for him." I vowed right then and there to avenge the pain that I'd caused my best friend by any means necessary.

We began to walk slowly inch by inch when we see Q wipe his face and stand to his feet. Ryder tries to walk back to where Q is but we stop him again. "He's still not ready yet. He'll let you know when he's ready."

When Quincy finally catches up to us he says, "If any one of you niggas repeat what you seen, I'm a kill ya."

We all shrug our shoulders and say, "Seen what?"

After Quincy was feeling a little better, he taps Jaylen and I on the shoulders and says, "Watch this." He laughs a little first and says, "GAYBOYSAYSWHAAAT!"

Jaylen and I remain silent and Ryder turns around and says, "W-what?" For a moment, we all forget what had just taken place. All the drama. All the disappointment. We laugh as if none of that had ever happened. But only for a moment.

Seeing the car in sight, we began to discuss who were going to walk to the gas station and get the gas after getting the gas can from the car. Quincy opted out and told the three of us to go so he could have some more time to think about things as he sat in the car.

Ryder stops dead in his tracks and yells, "I'M N-N-NOT GAY!" He had just gotten Quincy's joke. We just shake our heads on his slowness and I fumble around in my pockets searching for the car keys.

"Nigga! Come on, I just want to get home right now!" Quincy was becoming impatient.

"Hold up. I can't find the keys."

"That's because you left them still in the ignition." Quincy sits on the curb and drops his head.

24 CHAPTER TWENTY-FOUR
HUNTER SANTOS

I smile all the time so that nobody knows how sad & lonely I really am.

PAPI HAD TAKEN ALL the boys out to a birthday party at Chuck E. Cheese. So it was just Mami, me and Josiah. Symphony just called a minute ago. She wanted to come by and talk. Said what she wanted to talk about couldn't be text or spoken about over the phone. I was a little nervous because I now wondered if somehow she found out about Roman staying over here. She could be so possessive and clingy. That's probably why Roman never fully committed to her.

The closer that time ticked by, I wanted to cancel the whole thing. I didn't feel like dealing with this petty childish stuff. I'm going to just call and tell her not to come because I don't feel well. I dial her cell and she picks it up before it could even finish with the first ring.

"What?"

I take the phone away from my ear and look at it as if it just offended me. "Why you got to answer like that?" I ask Symphony.

"Because it's my phone and I can."

See? Her funky attitude. I can't deal with this right now. After changing Josiah's diaper I tickle his belly and he laughs. "Um, let's just do this another time. I'm not feeling too well."

"You look fine to me."

I turn around and she's standing in my bedroom doorway with the phone to her ear. I look at her, hang up my cell, and toss it onto the bed. Great! Let's just get this over with. She waltzes in my room, takes her jacket off, and sits in my chair. What I didn't know what that she was going to bring Spirit with her. "Hey, Spirit, what's up?"

"Girl! Have we got some stuff to tell you!" Spirit prances in and plops down on my bed startling Josiah.

"Spirit shut up! It ain't even your story to tell. You wasn't even there." Symphony laughs as she crosses her legs. I'm sure just to show off her cobalt Burberry jeans and her suede laced-ankle Manolo Pumps. She just wanted someone to tell her how hot they were. Well, I refuse to. I couldn't help but feel a little self-conscience with my hair in a messy ponytail and dried baby food glued to my t-shirt.

"Well you better tell her if you don't want me to." Spirit rocks her head back and forth.

"Tell me what?" All this back and forth and nobody saying anything had aroused my curiosity.

"Ok, so… you know we hooked up with Roman'em last night right?"

"Who?" I asked because she was being kind of vague on who the "we" was. Symphony stops and stares at me as if she was at a loss for words. "What?" I ask her.

"Did you even bathe today?"

"What?" I smell my armpits and they were good so I don't know what she was talking about.

"Because…" She stops again and wiggle her finger my way as if she was sprinkling pixie dust on me or something. "You got this housewife thing going on. It's not cute at all. Have you worn that t-shirt all weekend?"

I roll my eyes at her. I mean yeah, okay maybe I did but it was still clean and I did shower. I just put it back on. It's not like it was musty or anything. The food stains just came from JoJo today. I didn't go anywhere in it. "No I haven't worn this t-shirt all weekend. Go on with what you were saying and leave my attire out of it."

Symphony makes a face at me as if I were lying and continue to just stare at me. Or maybe she was staring at JoJo. I dunno.

"Oh forget it! Girl that chick was kissing and hugged up on your man the whole time!" Spirit exhaled as if she was holding her breath for hours.

I look at Spirit and say, "What chick?" Then I look at Symphony for the answer.

"As if you don't know." Symphony uncrosses her legs and readjust herself in my chair.

"No I don't know." I think for a moment and then say, "Amber?"

"Yup! Y'alls little lunch buddy."

"Oh." I don't know. I didn't have much feeling about that. Spirit and Symphony looks at me as if maybe I didn't hear or understand what they just said. I don't know if I didn't really react because I thought she was here about Roman or what.

"Oh?" Symphony questions. "So a chick all up on your man and all you have to say is Oh?"

"Well, Symphony what did you do?"

"I told her to get up off your man."

"Yup! But she didn't listen."

"Spirit shut up!" Symphony and I said in agreement.

"You betta' watch your man around that girl if you want him because I can tell she real thirsty."

I sigh and run my hands through my hair. I really don't have time for this. I throw my hands up. "Whatever. I'm sure he was doing more than that when I was gone."

"Shoot he was doing the mess when you were still here. And in your face!"

"Spirit shut up!" We both say again.

Spirit doesn't shut up, instead she continues to tell me that story of how they got caught by the cops and how Q gave Amber his weed and told her to run with it. Better her than me. Quincy already knows I don't play that mess. I do a reenactment as I spoke. "If it was me, I'd be like excuse me officer but he's holding and tried to give it to me to run with, officer sir." They laughed. I forced myself to laugh. We talked some more but I just wasn't in the haha life is fun and carefree mood but I wasn't going to show them that.

"Oh my goodness he's such a cutie." Spirit holds Josiah up as she plays with him. "Isn't he Symphony?"

She didn't say anything. She mumbles something that resembles "mhm."

"It's time for him to eat." Mami comes in and says as she grabs Josiah from Spirit. She cuts her eyes at me as if she's mad and wants me to do it.

Symphony stands up and the bangles on her arm jiggles. "It's time for us to go. Plus I know you're not feeling well and all."

I roll my eyes at her being sarcastic. "What? I don't."

"I know. You don't look all that well either."

♥♥♥

I'm glad they left. She just wanted to rub it in my face that they all went out last night and Quincy was up to his same old tricks. Little do she know I had her man in my bed the other night anyway. Humph, getting caught by the police didn't sound like fun to me. I'm glad I didn't go. Then she wanted to talk about what happened last year. Gave me her lame attempt at an apology from that time we were on the bus and how she blurted out that I left because I couldn't take the breakup of me and Q. Ha! Hardly… if she only knew.

She claimed I had changed. That I wasn't as fun to be around anymore.

Nah, I didn't change. I grew up… that's what all of them need to do… grow up. I thought about when Mami came and confronted me about Papi's whereabouts that night. How dare he have me cover for him. I still did it… but how dare he all the same. Till this day, I still don't know where he was, I don't really care. I just hate lying so much. It feels like something is on the inside eating away at me every day. I want to tell the truth so bad. But I know I can't. That's why I just stay away from people.

When I look around, my mother had Josiah dressed in some mixed matched clothes looking like a bums baby. "Mami… what are you doing?" I take Josiah from her and start removing his clothes.

"Why did you have her over here?"

"What do you mean?" This whole thing was starting to irritate me. "How can I keep making excuses to not have her come over here? We're best friends."

"You were best friends, Hunter…. Were!" She walked into the kitchen to start doing dishes and I followed with Josiah in my arms. "There is no way that you can lie and cheat a person and still say best friends."

"Well I wouldn't be lying but you're making me—"

"I'm making you!" She whirled around and slung soapsuds all over me and Josiah. "Did I make you sleep around with that girl's boyfriend? "Did I make you get pregnant by him?"

I tried to get up and walk away but she slammed be back into the chair. "You don't know what it's like Mami! Yeah I made a mistake… I got pregnant… Okay! So what… lots of girls do! But I'm not allowed to have my baby!" I began to cry hysterically. This tension has been building for a long time. After I told my mother I was pregnant and didn't know who the father was, we never spoke of it again. She and I packed up and moved out of state with my grandmother. I was never to tell anyone I was ever pregnant, not even my little brothers. The only people who ever knew was me, my parents and my grandmother… but she's gone now.

"Get out of my eyesight!" I took the invitation and ran into my room.

I was fuming! My mother just didn't understand. She didn't care what I was going through. All she thinks about is herself. I laid Josiah in his crib, propped his bottle on a pillow and let him feed himself.

My father and I used to have a great father daughter relationship until I got pregnant. When I first got pregnant, the first person I told was my mother. I don't even think I told symphony. See again, if she was my friend all like that… maybe I would have told her first. Anyway, when I told my mom, I was too far along to have an abortion. I was hiding it from everybody. Q couldn't tell because I'd stop sleeping with him when he started saying I was getting fat.

Anyway, my mother came up with this idea that since she needed to go take care of my sick grandmother out of state, that I'd go with her and she'd leave the boys with Papi. We didn't really have a plan, couldn't really stomach the thought of adoption either. Before we knew it, the baby was born and my abuela had passed. It was so fast it was like my grandmother and Josiah both switched places. Mami was meaning to tell Papi but with grandmother's death, her and dad's marital problems… it just got pushed to the back.

Before we even knew it, my father and the boys were knocking on the door and we hadn't even come up with anything yet about the baby. He walks in the house and there was this new edition that he didn't know anything about.

Mami told him the truth of course, but not the boys… we all thought it was best if they just thought the baby was their brother instead of their nephew. Well they thought it was best. I didn't have a choice but to go with it.

Right after the funeral, Papi took the boys and hightailed it back home, leaving my mother, JoJo, and I to fend for ourselves. We had to get grandmother's affairs in order anyways. I finished my homeschooling there and we made it back home by late summer.

It was crazy how I'd been gone for about a year. I still talked to everybody at home every now and then… but when I got back, everyone was still in the same place doing the same thing. It's like we all just picked back up our "friendship" as if I'd never left. Symphony and I were still "BFF's", Quincy and I were still "Boyfriend/Girlfriend", and Roman acted as if we'd never slept together.

Here I was, I had this big life-changing event. Going through actual grown people's issues and problems… and everyone is still out here playing and having fun sleeping around with no cares at all.

I hate her! I hate this whole stupid life! I can't wait until I'm 18! I pick up my cell and hold it in my hand contemplating on if I should just call Roman and tell him the whole truth and nothing but. Forget my parents. What were they going to do? Throw me out? I'd be glad if they did! I dialed Roman's number. Dangit! It went straight to his voicemail. Should I leave a message? Nah… that's not something you want to tell someone by recording. I'll just wait a few more minutes and call him back.

I hear a sneeze and look at me window. It was Spirit standing there looking back at me. "What are you doing?"

"Uh, I came back to get Symphony's jacket… but then I heard you guys arguing and I decided I'd wait it out."

"You mean you thought you'd just sit there and listen to it all!" Spirit just continues to stand there with her mouth open. "If you ever tell anybody…"

♥♥♥

NOVEMBER

25 CHAPTER TWENTY-FIVE
AMBER STYLES

How people treat you is their karma; how you react is yours. ~Wayne Dyer

"HERE YOU GO MS. Joi."

I sat at the kitchen table eating my grilled cheese sandwich when Willow comes in and hands my mom a garbage bag.

"Oh thank you sweetie." My mom sounded so fake. "Amber tell Willow thank you."

"For what?" I said with as much attitude that wouldn't cause me to get backhanded.

"For giving you all these clothes, that's for what."

I suck my teeth. "Please! I ain't about to be thankful for nobody's garbage! I ain't wearing that!" My mom had a lot of nerves. Willow do have some nice stuff but please... I ain't about to take nothing from no snitch. Plus she trying to be funny by putting it in a garbage bag! She needs to roll with all that! She just mad because I ain't kiss her butt. I kept rolling my eyes at her every time she looked my way.

"It's ok Ms. Joi... I don't need a thank you."

"Well Amber can be ungrateful all she wants to. I sure thank you for this. Hey, why don't you take Amber to the mall with you? Maybe you guys can talk and get rid of all this animosity."

"Sure. I don't mind. If she wants to. We were just going to the mall to do a little shopping and find me a dress for Winter Formal."

"Yeah right! I ain't going nowhere with that snitch!" Now this heffa wants to throw it in my face that she's going to Winter Formal and I'm not because I'm on punishment.

"Don't make me come over there and yank ya little ass up! It's time for all that sassiness to seize and desist. Do you understand me?"

"Yeah." I say with more attitude than I meant to.

My mom comes all up in my face. "Yeah? Since when do you answer me with yeah?"

"Yes…"

"Yes what?"

"Yes ma'am." I felt like I was in the army and she was my drill Sargent instead of my mother.

♥♥♥

I feel like a dang fool at the mall being Willow's tag along. It just felt like her and her mom was being a little too extra. All of a sudden, her mom took my so-called best friend. They were walking together and laughing, talking, running in and out of stores.

When we get into Macy's, I ditch the new BFF's and find myself drifting into the MAC section. It was so many people in there, it was nuts. I browse around the store looking at all the different make-up and colors. I wonder if I could find that troublemaker lipstick and see how much it cost. Thirty-five dollars!? And that's supposed to be a sale? I almost ran out of there.

As I turn to go back down the aisle to leave, the same little white boy with red hair and freckles kept tugging on my purse straps. "Where's your mother?" I whisper to him. I figure he must be lost. Ever since I first came in the store, he's been following and bumping into me… dang near walking on my heels. So annoying. Anyway, he didn't say anything. Just keeps looking at me. My eyes roam the store looking for any woman with red hair that may resemble the little redhead boy.

I almost didn't want to leave the store without finding who his mother was. Maybe if I browse a little more he might walk away and attach himself to somebody else. I browse the foundation stuff some more wondering which shade was my shade. It was so many. Different shades and shades that dang near looked the same. I would pick some up, read the color, and put it back. BUMP… OMG! Where is this kid's mom? Everywhere I go he follows me, bumping me.

"Samuel there you are! Get over here!"

It's about time. He waves bye to me and run to his mother. I guess that was her over there getting a free makeover the whole time. I need to come here and get my makeup done for free. I wonder how many times they let you do that? People can come here every day without even buying this make up. I see Willow and her mom waving me over. I take one glance around as I leave. I love this store. I will be back someday.

I was getting bored and tired walking around and watching her buy clothes and trying on this and that. I ain't never bought nothing from the mall. I browse around the racks and look at the prices. Now I see why my mother never brings me here to buy stuff, these prices are outrageous!

"Oh come on Amber! Try on some of this with me." I look at Willow as if she lost her mind. "Come on… lighten up and have some fun."

How the heck she figure this is fun for me? She stuffs like three dresses in my hand. Fine. I browse the racks and found a cute fuchsia color short strapless dress with diamonds all over it. All the dresses that Willow handed me where all big and bulky and fell all the way to the floor like something a princess would wear. The tags on the dresses were over a hundred dollars. Except the one, I picked. It was on the clearance rack and was marked down like three times, all the way to twenty-five dollars.

I wonder why nobody wants this dress? It was cute to me. I began to feel sorry for the dress. It was weird because it was a dress. It didn't have any feelings. But still. Somehow, I compared the dress to me. I sympathized with it. Understood how it was unwanted. Unloved. Lonely. Reduced down multiple times to nothing. Yet and still it never stood a chance next to all these bigger more extravagant dresses. The dress, like me, was an outcast.

The changing room sections says, "Limit 3," I want to put one of the dresses that Willow gave me back so I could as least try the little pink dress on. Let it know that someone did care about it. But Willow was looking at me. I slide the pink dress in-between the other bigger dresses and it disappears.

The first dress I try on is the little lonely pink dress. It fits perfectly. It was beautiful. I stay in there the whole time admiring myself in the mirror with it on. O well. I take it off and toss it to the side with my purse. The dang thing was so thin, it darn near slipped inside. I go over to hang it back on the hanger.

Removing the dress from my purse, I peer in and find out it wasn't the only thing that had slipped in there. Mr. Baby Bumps was hooking me up the whole time! I had dang near a bag full of MAC cosmetics. My heart dropped when I had seen this. I didn't know whether to go back to the store and tell them what happened, or take my blessings and run.

Wait, was that a blessing? On the other hand, was it stealing? At this point, I was confused on what side of the commandments I was on. Maybe it was a sign. Maybe God wanted me to have these things. Why not? I look at the little pink dress in my hands. It didn't even have one of those detector thingies. Before I knew it, I snatch the tag off and slide the little pink dress into my bag. I didn't even bother to try on any of the other ones. Still confused on how wrong I was, I prayed to God to get me out of the store safe and sound.

"You didn't like any of the dresses Amber?" Willow's mom ask me as she was fiddling around with the dress that Willow was trying on.

What do you care if I liked any of the dresses or not! It wasn't like I was going to Winter Formal or as if you were going to buy me a dress! That's what I wanted to say, but instead, I just said, "No ma'am." I didn't want to be in this store any more. I didn't even want to be in the mall! The stuff I had in my purse was so hot it was burning a hole in the bottom. I try to keep myself from thinking the worse. From me going out the door and the alarm going off. "May I have the keys to the car, Ms. Kathy, I'm not feeling too well."

She feels my forehead like I was a toddler or something and she was checking for a fever. Really! I wanted to say. She gives me the keys and tells me how to turn the key enough to roll the windows down but to make sure I take them out right after and not to turn the car on. Duh! I think to myself.

I felt like I was taking a walk on the wild side. The closer I approach the exit my heart thumps a little louder… harder… faster. I was fighting with my legs not to run. No no no! Slow down! You're drawing attention to yourself. You're doing like a walk jog now… that's still too fast… you're making it look like your limping… stop it! Remember… slow and steady wins the race… come on girl! Where's your confidence? You own this store! Yeah… this is your business, you were just coming to check on your employees… yeah there ya go… slow it down… easy…. easy…. I say a quick prayer to the Lord that if He gets me out of this, I'd never steal again in my life. I take a step over the threshold… that's one foot…. Two feet…. Now bring the purse around…. YES! You did it! You're out the door and on your way out the mall!!! Once you're in the car, your home scot-free!

26 CHAPTER TWENTY-SIX

Dear karma, I have a list of people you forgot.

"NO, NO, NO, NO, No!" Cam'Ron trashes his room in search of the Jordan's but no matter how hard he looked the results were still the same.

"What are you doing?" Amber's eyes bulge as she sees Cam'Ron's room in shambles. "Oooh! Mommy's going to get you!"

"Shut up! Have you seen 'em?" Cam'Ron runs up to Amber and grabs her by the arms.

"Seen what?"

"The shoes!"

"What shoes?"

"Ugh!" Cam'Ron pushes Amber aside and runs into her room ready and willing to destroy it too.

"Get out of my room, Cam!" Amber yells and tries her best to stop Cam'Ron.

"Help me find them then."

"Okay! But get out of my room, they're not in here!"

The siblings tussle as Cam'Ron rips the sheets off Amber's mattress and throws everything from under her bed. "Mom!"

Joi appears in Amber's doorway. "What the hell is going on?"

"He's tearing up the house because he says he can't find some dumb shoes."

"Well why didn't you ask me? I can tell you where they are?"

Cam'Ron runs up to his mother, "Where?"

"The dumpster."

"What!" He throws his hands into the air. "Oh my god! You have got to be kidding me! Why would you do that?"

"Because those damn shoes were stankin' up the house. I don't see how you were wearing them things every day. No wonder your friend gave them to you. Smells like a skunk died in them."

Cam'Ron stumps past his mother and into his room to throw on some clothes so he could go dumpster diving, all the while throwing obscenities at his mother under his breath. Cam'Ron bolts past his mother and out the door with only socks on his feet when he hears screeching sounds. "Don't even think about bringing them shoes back up in here!" Joi yells to Cam'Ron. The garbage truck was making its way out of their parkway and onto the street.

"Wait!" Cam'Ron yells as he takes off full speed after the truck. "Wait!" His feet flapping and smacking the concrete with each stride. As the truck turns the corner and is out of Cam'Ron's sight, he slows down to a stop, and drops his head. He has given up. It was useless. They didn't hear him. He doubts that they even cared.

Cam'Ron stands at the corner panting and trying to catch his breath when he noticed that he'd run all the way to "The Bottom." Not a place he wanted to be especially without the Jordan's on. He only had a few more days to go before his two months of wearing the pissy shoes were up. You'd think the Walkers would let it go, but they wouldn't.

Cam'Ron hears booming bass approaching and knows it's Remy's car coming from around the corner. He looks down at his feet and takes off running again. He runs through yards and cuts through apartments as he hears the beeping horn of Remy's car. His heart is pumping in overdrive but so is his adrenaline. He knows they see him and will eventually catch him without the shoes on his feet. He cuts through the side of a house and runs smack dap into someone.

"Yo, slow down bruh. You wouldn't happen to be running from Patrón and Remy now would you?" Roman couldn't help but gloat a bit at this moment.

"Get out my way!" Cam'Ron tries to maneuver himself around Roman because he could hear the music getting closer and closer.

"Where you going?"

"Home, nigga!"

"Hmm… I don't know about that one seeing as though that's probably them about to pull up now." Roman pulls his hand from behind his back and hands Cam'Ron the shoes.

"Bruh!" Cam'Ron snatches the shoes and places them on his feet with the quickness. "How?"

"Oh, I'm your bruh now huh? I seen your mom when she threw them in the dumpster."

"So you went dumpster diving for me?"

"Hell naw. The dumpster was full so she sat them on top of all the trash. I just picked them up. Thought you'd still need them seeing how the two months aren't quite up yet."

"Man, good lookin' out. I owe you."

Remy pulls up and sees Roman and Cam'Ron in between the houses talking. He looks down at Cam'Ron's feet and says, "I could have sworn I saw the bottom of your dirty ass socks when you were running."

"Huh? Nah, not me." Cam'Ron answers and throws his head back and silently thanks God as he see Remy pull off.

"Have you even washed those things man?"

"Yeah I washed them. A lot of good it did though."

♥♥♥

Spirit sat in the lunchroom with her straw pressed against her lips as she stared into another dimension. Holding on to Hunter's secret… a secret of this magnitude was enough to make her spontaneously combust. You don't know how many times she came so close to telling Symphony. Spirit will be the first to admit that she loves getting the scoop and rundown on people and sharing it with others and swearing them to secrecy. But this time the shoe was on the other foot, Hunter had sworn her to secrecy and it didn't feel good at all. She tried. But she wasn't so sure she could keep it for much longer.

Jaylen waves his hand in front of Spirit's face to make her snap back to reality. "What are you thinking about?"

Spirit looks at Jaylen and her soul moans. She begins to wrestle with herself. Should she tell or nah? "J?"

"Yea?" Jaylen squirts ketchup onto his hamburger.

"I need to talk to you." Jaylen sighs and looks at Spirit. "Trust me, it's nothing like that. It's not gossip or anything. Or is it?"

"O, boy."

Spirit begins to give Jaylen the rundown of how she overheard Hunter and her mother arguing a few days ago. Jaylen holds his hand up to stop Spirit from talking. "I don't want to hear it! Spirit you were eavesdropping."

"No I wasn't. Not on purpose. You have to let me finish if you want to understand what I'm dealing with, Jaylen. It involves something serious about your cousin."

"Who Ro?" Spirit looks at Jaylen as if saying who else. "Nah, I still don't think I want to know."

"Hunter's baby brother is really her son!" Spirit exhaled and it felt like Mount Rushmore had fell off her shoulders. She stuffed three fries in her mouth at once and began to chew slowing enjoying every bit of it as it slid down her throat. These few days has left her only eating to survive. She hasn't enjoyed a meal in days.

"Even if that was true, what's that have to do with my cousin? Sounds like a Quincy problem to me." Spirit choked on her milk and told Jaylen everything. "Nope. That doesn't sound right. If what you're saying is true, you're saying my cousin is a liar and a cheat. A double cheat at that because he cheated on Symphony and his best friend."

"I'm not saying anything!" Spirit began to get offended. "I'm just repeating what I heard from the horse's mouth."

"That's your problem Spirit! You always repeating something you have no business knowing in the first place." Jaylen slams his chocolate milk carton onto his tray and milk squirts on the table.

"Are you going to tell them?"

"Tell who?"

"Symphony? Roman?"

"Hell no! Why would I do that when I don't even believe none of it in the first place?"

"So you calling me a liar?"

Jaylen scoots his tray in the middle of the table not even bothering to throw it away. He looks at Spirit, places his hoodie on his head, and walks out the cafeteria.

♥♥♥

Symphony's mother let her use the car to run to the grocery store to pick up a few things for dinner. She took Harmony with her because she was crying and begging to go. Symphony has her driver's license. Actually, it was more as a birthday gift because she passed the test on her 16th birthday. And on the first try. She's a good driver. Responsible and legal. The only one in the squad who has them.

Sure, she could ask her mother to drive the car when Roman and she plan to do something, but if Roman is going to be her man, Symphony wanted him to act like a man. He needs to get a job, get his license, and buy his own car because she would like to be wined and dined sometimes instead of just going to the movies on his allowance.

"Harmony stop that!" Symphony yells as she sees Harmony throwing groceries into a random stranger's grocery cart. Symphony reaches in the stranger's cart to get it out.

"All this stuff in the store and you have to shop from my cart?" Symphony jumps back because the deep male voice had startled her.

"Mommy! I want fruit snacks."

"Aww, your daughter is so precious." Mr. Random goes over, pinches Harmony's plump cheeks, and hands her the Dora the Explorer fruit snack she had thrown into his cart.

"She's my sister." He looks up at Symphony and she notices he has hazel eyes. She begins to check him out from head to toe.

"No need to be ashamed. I could see if you were still in high school." Symphony wasn't sure if this guy was joking or not.

"How old do you think I am?" Symphony places her hands on her hips and shifts her weight to one side. Now's he's checking her out. Not a problem because she already knew everything was already on point. It's a habit whenever she step out of bed to make sure the hygiene and looks are fly and stays that way throughout the day.

"I'd say about 19-21." Symphony laughs because his tone and demeanor was as if he knew he was correct. She just let it go because it wasn't like she was going to see him again. "What's your name?"

"Symphony… why?"

He extends his hand to her and says, "What a beautiful name, for a beautiful lady. Nice to meet you, I'm the King."

She looks at his hand as if he had a booger on it. No matter how fine this dude was he just turned 100% ugly to her. She begins to push the shopping cart Harmony sat in and walk away.

"Hold on. Did I do or say something to offend you?"

"You don't even know me and you're going to sit up here and introduce yourself to me as "the king"? Boy bye!" Symphony rolls her eyes and keeps it moving. When Symphony looks back, he was standing there busting a gut as if she was the female version of Kevin Hart.

"Okay, okay." He holds his abs to control his laughter, then reaches into his pocket, and pulls out his wallet. She was really about to walk then because she knows he was not trying to solicit her in the grocery store, or anywhere for that matter!

He pulls out his Driver's license and Symphony feels so stupid. His name was DeKing Washington. He gave Symphony his business card with his number and told her to give him a call and that he'd love to take her out to dinner or even invite her over so he could cook for her. She'd be lying if she said she wasn't the least bit interested. For the rest of the day, Symphony felt a tinge of guilt every time she thought about DeKing Washington.

27 CHAPTER TWENTY-SEVEN
ROMAN DAVIS

Any woman can give birth, but it takes a special person to be a real mother.

I CONTEMPLATED EVERYDAY IF I should snoop and read those letters. I had been tempted a couple of times because big head Q can't leave it alone. If I didn't know any better you'd think we were talking about his mother instead of mine.

I've sat here day after day, wondering why was she locked up and why no one has ever told me. Why did Ma keep this secret from me? What made her think that telling me a lie would be better than the truth? It made me wonder what could be worse than, 'Your mom left you here with me because she didn't love you.'

I had so many questions running through my head that it was getting hard to sleep at night and concentrate on schoolwork. Why was my mother in jail? I replayed confronting Ma, repeatedly in my head and each time no good came out of any of the scenarios.

I thought about talking to Symphony but she seemed to be preoccupied lately. No way was I talking to Q's nosey butt, spreading my business everywhere. I'm surprised he hasn't said anything to anyone about the letters. On second thought, maybe I will talk to Q. He could be maturing since he has kept his mouth shut.

"What's up?" Jaylen comes into my room and leans up against the wall.

"Sup." I remove my ear buds and sit on the edge of my bed. The room was silent until Jaylen spoke again.

"So, was you ever goin' tell me?"

"Tell you what? Jaylen just stands there and stares at me as if I should know what he's talking about.

"About the letters. What else?"

Ain't this something! I take back any mature thought I just had about Quincy. "What you need me to tell you for when you already got a snitch buddy?"

"So, that how it is?"

"It's however you want it."

Silence filled the air again so I ignore Jaylen and start playing my PlayStation. I turn the sound down low as to not be so rude. I know it's not Jaylen's fault.

"Was it anything in there from my mom?"

"I don't know."

"What you mean you don't know?"

"Nigga, just what I said! I-don't-know!" He was starting to get out of the pocket with the tone of his voice. "I haven't read any of them yet."

He storms out of my room like a mad two-year old. *Man whatever! Bounce with all that.* It just all mad nonsense. After a few minutes had passed, I got nosey and wondered what he was up to. I found him in Ma's room fumbling around in the closet.

"Yo man, what you doing?"

"What it look like?"

I really don't know what this dude's problem is but he had better check himself before we be fist to cuffs.

"Where y'all at?" I hear Ma yells as she walks up the steps. We hurry and I help Jaylen shove the box back into the closet and we run to Jaylen's room because it was the closest.

She peeks her head in the door, "Y'all get ready to come down and eat. I brought back some Church's Chicken."

"Okay Grandma, we'll be down." After Ma left Jaylen's room, he say, "How come you ain't tell me though?"

I ask him how come he ain't never tell me where he seen ole dude from. He doesn't answer so I get ready to leave out the door and head downstairs to eat.

"Okay, okay… close the door back." I close the door and give him my full attention. "In my dreams."

"What?"

"I seen him… in my dreams."

"What is you gay now?"

He waves me off now because he's mad I was making fun of him. Well if he was going to play games so was I. He curls up on his bed and pulls out one of the letter he must have stuff into his pocket. I go to grab it and he snatches it away. We wrestle and fight over it a bit and as soon as I get the letter in my hand, Ma opens the door.

"Quit all that playing around and get on down here because after I wash them dishes up the kitchen is closed. Y'all here me?"

"Yes ma'am." We both say in unison.

Jaylen snatches the letter back and places it under his pillow and we both head downstairs to eat.

It took Jaylen and me less than 5 minutes to eat two thighs each, fried okra, mash potatoes & gravy, and a biscuit. We threw our bones in the trash and put our plates in the sink so we both could hurry back upstairs to read that letter.

"Un unn... Y'all better high-tail y'alls butts back down here and help me." *Man,... she buggin'.* "Y'all so in a hurry to play that dang game. Ro, help me with the dishes. J, wipe the table down, sweep the floor, and take that trash out." Man! I know it sounds like Jaylen had more to do but his would take no time. I however had dishes to do from yesterday! And Ma know when she says help me, she really means do it for me.

Jaylen was done with his work so I had to dang near beg him to help me by rinsing. Within a half hour we were upstairs and opening the letter to read it.

Dear momma,

I don't know how many times I have to apologize or what I have to do or how many years has to go by before you accept my apology and forgive me.

How is my son? You do tell him about me don't you? Please tell him I love him and think about him every day.

I know you probably won't write back because you never do... I just hope everything is okay with you and lil' Ro.

Tears began to swell up in my eyes and believe it or not, I wanted to cry. I don't know nothing about my mother. I don't even know what she looks like. Ma don't have no pictures around here of either of our mothers.

"You think she's hiding something in that box about my mother?" I wanted to say whatever it was that Jaylen wanted to hear. I wanted him to have some kind of hope that I now had. I wanted to believe that my mother did love me. But for some reason, Ma—my grandmother, was lying and hiding it from me. What could my mother have done that was so bad that would make my grandma lie and not forgive her own daughter?

"It's gotta be J. You see all that stuff in there?" Jaylen nods his head. "Its gotta be… she has to be lying about yours too."

"You think my mom could be in jail too… like yours?"

"I don't know J… I don't know. But whatever it is Ma has got to know something. They were sisters."

♥♥♥

DECEMBER

28 CHAPTER TWENTY-EIGHT HUNTER SANTOS

The naked truth is always better than someone's best dressed lie.

"I can't go."

"Quit playin'."

"Does it sound like I'm playing Q?" I was already irritated and Quincy was making it worse. Something in my room smelled big time and I couldn't find out the source of it. "I told you I have to babysit. It's not like it's going to be the last dance ever."

"Then why in the hell you make me buy this monkey suit?"

"Un huh… don't put that on me. Every time you asked, I told you I didn't know yet."

"Aight… whatever. You want me to bring some drink over or something tonight?"

I take the phone away from my ear and contemplate throwing it. "What is it that you don't understand?"

"I'm just saying that since you can't go to Winter Formal, I won't go either. I can come over and spend some time."

"Quincy! I'm not having sex with you!"

"What! We haven't had sex in a whole year and then some!"

"So! I'm sure you've had your share with other females."

"You been with anybody else?"

"I'm not even going to answer that."

It was a long silence between us on the phone until Josiah woke up and started crying.

"Would you shut that baby up?"

"He's just a baby Quincy!"

"I don't give a damn, he all in my ear!"

You see what I'm saying, not one compassionate bone in his body. I'm glad he's not Josiah's father. I can't take this anymore, I am sick of dealing with Q's corny ass.

"You know what?"

"What?"

"I'm done."

"Done with what?"

"Done with this! With you!"

"Done with me? What, you saying that you don't want to be friends nomore?"

"I don't want to be in a relationship with you anymore."

Quincy began to laugh. "Relationship? What relationship, Hunter? In order to be in a relationship, you have to have relations."

"Well, you seem to be doing just fine in that department!"

"What you mean by that?"

"Really? Really Q? We gone play that game. Symphony told me!"

It was pure silence on the other end of the phone. I changed Josiah's diaper and then he said, "That was just one time. Why would she tell you that anyway?"

"Really? Just one time! You saying it like you and Amber hooked up or something."

"Amber?"

"Who the heck did you think I was talking about?"

"Naw, I knew you was talking about her."

"You know what? I don't even care, its over! Don't call me, text me, email me, Facebook me, or tweet me." I hung up the phone, logged onto my Facebook page, and changed my relationship status from "it's complicated" to "single".

♥♥♥

My mother had taken the boys to the market to pick up some food. Therefore, it was just Papi, Josiah, and me for a moment. Papi had just hopped out of the shower, so I figured it was a good enough time as any to finally hash it all out.

"Papi?" No answer. "Why won't you talk to me?" Then finally, he turned around and actually looked at me.

"Why do I need to waste my breath talking to you for?" It brought tears to my eyes and his words stung a bit but at least he was finally responding.

"Because, Papi, like you said, no matter how old I get, I will always be your little girl!"

"You're no little girl of mine. Any parts of a little girl I had flew out the window when she started giving her innocence to these little niggas in the street."

"Papi, don't say that? I lied to Mami for you!"

"So what! I lied for you when I didn't tell her you were laying up with the little nigga in my house!"

Dang! I've been so worried about this thing with Josiah that I forgot about asking Roman about that. "What did you say to him, Papi?"

"It don't matter what I said. This is my damn house and I pay the rent. You ain't no better than the rest of those fast ass heffas. Any daughter I had wouldn't have acted or done anything of what you've done."

"Papi, please forgive me. I'll make it up to you."

"What you've done is unforgiveable, now… I'm done talking."

♥♥♥

My father was so stupid. There are girls that has about 2-3 kids and they're only 12 years old. How long am I supposed to suffer because of one little stupid mistake. He needs to really get over it and let it go. I mean, it's serious but it ain't that serious.

Well, I hope everyone has a good time at Winter Formal tonight. I could have went if I wanted to but I just didn't feel like it. Everyone says I changed. That I'm different now. I can't say they're lying because I feel different. I just don't have the drive or the energy to do the things I used to do. I want to do things, go places, and kick it with my friends. I just don't feel like it.

I think I would be all right if Roman just knew about his son. Maybe then, some of this guilt would be lifted from my shoulders and I could breathe again. Roman is just so hard to get a hold of now. When I try to work up the nerve to tell him at school, she's always around him like a hound dog. I don't really want to call his phone, leave a voicemail, or text because you know you know who will be all up in it. I got real grown-up issues I'm dealing with. Why should I just let him off the hook scot-free and not tell him? He help create Josiah. I didn't do this on my own, so I shouldn't have to bear all the drama on my own either. Forget this, I'm about to call him and tell him. If she finds out, she just finds out.

I pick up my cell and dial his number but as usual he doesn't answer. I wonder if he doesn't answer because he knows it's me and he scared I'm going to ask him for something again. Even if that was the case, so what!

I'm so tempted to leave him a message or just text it to him. I bet you he'd call back real quick then. But what if I do that and Symphony go on her routine check of his phone and messages. Humph. It would serve her right if she did. She doesn't own him. Maybe I'll just call her first and see if they're together.

"Girl, I was just about to call you. Why you ain't going to Winter Formal?" She asked me without even saying hello.

"Dang! Quincy got a big mouth!"

"Well, that's something you should have told me yourself, don't you think? Plus you had me make your dress for nothing."

"I guess. But that's what I was calling you for." She uhn hun me like she didn't believe what I was saying. At this point, I could care less. "Well, you dressed?" I ask her trying to buy some time like I'm not trying to find out where her man is.

"Almost." She pops her gum into the receiver all in my ear smacking.

"What time y'all leaving?"

"Roman said he would be here about 5:30."

"5:30? Why so early?"

"Dayum girl, all up in mine!"

I ignore Symphony's last comment. All I really needed to know was if they were together or not and they weren't. "Alright. I'll let you finish getting dressed. I know y'all are going to upload some pics on Facebook." I tried to sound happy for them.

"Shut up… you suck!"

"I know. Have some fun for me too." I hang up and immediately dial Roman again. It went straight to voicemail. I was going to leave a message but I chickened out right when it was time for me to start speaking. I left him a text instead.

HEY ROMAN, THIS IS HUNTER… *delete that… he already knows it's me… duh!*

BEEN TRYING TO GET IN TOUCH WITH YOU SINCE FOREVER. BUT IT SEEMS LIKE UR AVOIDING MY CALLS.

I need to hurry this up and shorten it up. Roman don't like long text. He says if it's anything longer than the standard block he won't read it. Says if it's longer than that, it's a conversation and the person needs to call him.

At this point, my heart is beating out of my chest and my mind is running a mile a minute. Something is telling me not to do it and I'm strongly considering that voice… but I ignore it and continue.

WE NEED TO TLK. U RMBER MY BRO JOSIAH RIGHT? WELL… HES NO MY BRO. HE MY SON. OUR SON… I KNOW U HAVE A LOT OF ?'S… SO I GUESS WE WILL TLK WHEN U GET THE CHANCE… BTW…DON'T NOBODY NO… SO PLS KEEP THIS BETWEEN US.

I read over the text to make sure every things right. I hesitate pressing the send button. My fingers hover above the button contemplating. I think about my parents, I think about Roman, I think about Q, I think about Symphony… and I take my hand away from the send button. Contemplating erasing the message. Sitting on the edge of my bed, I can see a sleeping Josiah and myself in the mirror. He smiles in his sleep. I look at the text again… and press send.

I watch as the message load itself through the atmosphere and reaches its destination. "Oh No!" My eyes quickly scan the sent message again and I notice a mistake. "HES NO MY BRO." And a few other idiot mistakes. O well, it's too late now. I sit and wait like a prisoner on death row waiting for the Governor to call before the clock strikes twelve.

29 CHAPTER TWENTY-NINE
AMBER STYLES

The main reason why a daughter needs a dad is to show her that not all the boys are like the ones who hurt her.

I RODE WITH MY father over to my grandmother's house to drop Cam'Ron off. Granny Dot still lived in a huge 3-bedroom home where my mom mostly grew up. My mom's brother Leonard still lived with granny but you would never know because he was always gone. When he did come home, he was always stinking drunk and granny would have to use her walking cane to beat the devil out of him. At least that's what she tells me.

Since it was two flights of stairs to my grandmother's room, my mom and dad had turned the dining room into a bedroom for granny. She liked being on one floor and not having to climb all those stairs to go to bed in such a dark house. My mom had tried many times to get granny to down size and move into a smaller apartment but granny wasn't ready to let her house of memories go just yet. She said her beloved past away in this house and she was going to do the same.

Being respectful, I knock on my grandmother's door. "It opens!" Granny yells from her favorite chair in the living room.

"Hey Granny!" I walk over to hug her and my dad follows suit and did the same. Cam gives granny a quick kiss on the cheek and tells her he's about to go over his friend's house next door.

"Don't you stay too long now 'cause you know I can't come lookin' for you." He promises her he won't but dad and I both know that Cam never lives up to his promises. Granny looks at dad and says, "You come to car' me to my 'pointment?"

My dad had no idea granny had a doctor's appointment. "Ah, yeah I can mom, what time you supposed to be there?" He said scratching his head.

For some reason my name wouldn't come from granny's mouth. Not that she had forgotten who I was. "Uh... Uh... baby?" Granny said referring to me. "Hand me my, ah... pocketbook." I did as I was told. She reached inside and pulled out a business card with her appointment written in pen.

Granny placed her glasses on her face and bent her head forward to look out of the top of them. "Gosh darnit! I can't read this." I wanted to say... well granny if maybe if you tried looking through the glasses instead of out of the top of them. But I didn't. "What this here say?" Granny handed the card to me.

"It says, 2:30, Granny."

"Huh? 2:30?"

"Yes, ma'am."

"Uh huh. Yes. Well, what time is it now?"

My dad took a look at the card and noticed that the appointment was dated for last week. "Mama, this appointment was for last week. You're going to have to make another one. You're not going to be able to go today."

"Ah shucks. Well carry that card to Joi and tell her to make me a 'pointment, okay? I told Leonard bout my 'poinment but he don't never be here. I needs to get my medicine."

"I know mama, I'll have Joi make the next appointment as soon as possible and if Joi can't take you, I will."

"Okay, thank you son." Granny always thought my dad was a good man. She never understood why he and my mom had gotten a divorce. I heard she tried so hard to talk my mom out of it but once my mom gets her mind made up, it's no stopping her.

I thought it was a good time to ask my grandmother for a laptop. "Hey Granny?"

She was writing in her huge black diary as she often did. "Chile, I keep telling you that hay is for horses."

I laughed. "I'm sorry Granny." I went to sit on the floor next to her swollen feet. "Do you think you can get me a laptop?"

"Oh Chile, I don't know. You 'bout too big to be sittin' on top of 'ole granny's lap."

"No Granny. It's a computer."

"A 'puter? O no, I don't know nothing 'bout no 'puters Chile. You ask your mother?"

"I did but she said no."

"Well, if she said no, I'm sure it was for a reason." My grandmother and my father both shared a look at each other and smiled. I didn't think anything was funny at all.

"Daddy?"

"Nooo Amber. You know your mama is the Queen Bee. What she says goes. Besides, you know I don't have no money like that right now." He went on eating granny's famous pound cake.

"Well what about a cell phone?" I begged.

"What do you need with a cell phone Amber?"

I give up, grab my coat, and ran outside onto my grandmother's porch. It was a little chilly but not freezing, thank God. I sit on the steps and wanted to cry like a baby because no one understood me or what I was going through. I was tired of hearing about how everyone is broke and how I can't have this or that. It made me angry that everyone else in the world seemed to have something and get to enjoy life except me. It just wasn't fair!

♥♥♥

As if to make matters worse, I'm at my dad's house and I finally meet his "friend." That's what he calls her. Already I'm not sure if I like her or not. He tells me that he just got called into work. So much for daughter daddy time.

"Why can't I just go stay with granny?"

"Well for one, Amber, you're already here."

"I can go home and stay by myself, daddy."

"No, I don't want to hear your mom's mouth. If it were up to me, I'd say you were old enough to watch yourself. But for now, just stay here with Melissa.

"Fine." I went into the living room and started watching T.V. I flicked through over 300 channels and still haven't found anything to watch. It's so boring here. I should have stayed at my grandmother's while I still had the chance.

♥♥♥

I'm sitting in my dad's basement talking to his female "Friend." I guess she's not as bad as I thought. She looks white but she acts black. I laugh inside every time she speaks. I close my eyes when she talks and could swear up and down she was darker than I was. I guess she's cute. She has a nice shape for a white girl. (*No lesbo*) I wonder how old she is but I'm scared to ask because I think that would be rude, but I do it anyway.

"How old is you?" She was about to take a sip of her drink and then stopped before it touched her thin lips.

"I'm twenty-five." She stares at me for a reaction. It takes me a minute to do the math. I have to use my fingers a little bit and hope she doesn't notice.

"OMG! You're like, twelve years younger than my dad?"

"Yeah, I know right." She takes another sip of her drink and asks me if I mind if she lit a cigarette. I don't care what she does. I think about that night Symphony let me smoke hers and how I choked to death. I'm wiggling my fingers again against my jeans.

"Hold up! Your only ten years older than me!"

"Yep…"

Hmmm… I'm thinking my mom might be salty if she knew daddy had a younger woman, even though I know she's seeing Keith. "How long have you been smoking?"

"Geesh… I'm almost embarrassed to say. Russell might think I'm a bad influence on his baby girl."

"Please! I'm hardly a baby. I'm fifteen."

"I know and I was only two years younger than you when I first started smoking."

Dangit! What is she, a dang math teacher? Why can't she just say a dang number? I tap my fingers again against my leg. I ain't that dumb, but I had to check to make sure I was right.

"Can you teach me?"

"Girl, you must want your daddy to kill me!"

"He ain't gotta know."

"What the hell! But keep it between us okay?"

She lights another cigarette, hands it to me, and shows me what to do. I follow her instructions to the 'T' and I don't choke. I'm blowing rings in the air and having it flow from my mouth straight into my nose. Ok, I admit that burned and I choked a little. I don't like doing it that way but the rings are cool. She was even letting me drink some of daddy's liquor. I'ma have to hang out more often with her. I was feeling empowered like I could conquer anything.

"So, how come you not allowed to go to Winter Formal?" I told her the whole story of me sneaking out and what all went down. "Awww… that messed up. She could have at least let you go to your first Winter Formal."

"Oh, I know… and I had my dress and everything." I pulled the dress out of my bag and showed her. Don't ask why I still had the dress in there. I haven't found a good hiding place for it yet. Plus, I like taking it out every now and then and looking at it.

"Wow, this is hot!" She hands it back to me. "Here… go try it on." She ain't have to ask me twice. I ran to the bathroom and put the dress on. By the time I opened the door to come out Melissa was standing there with three pairs of heels, jewelry, and wigs. We were having a ball playing dress up. She put my make-up on better than Symphony. I put on one of her long black wigs with chinky china bangs. At first, I was like, how I'm gone do that when you got white girl hair. But she was right, this looked like black girl weave or something. Not only did I look like a model, I felt like one.

My ugly cheap Obama phone started ringing. I know it had to be my mom, probably sensing I was having fun and she's trying to put an end to it. I almost didn't answer it but I know she would be over here in a flash if I didn't.

"Hello." I said with much attitude.

"Dang baby… if it's all like that you want to hit me back?" *OMG! I know this ain't who I think it is.*

"Who dis?" I ain't goin' lie y'all, I'm tipsy as heck right now.

"Quit trippin' girl, you know this Q."

"Oh, hey Q." I tried to act like I didn't really care that much that he was calling me. I pointed to the phone to let Melissa know that this was one of the dudes I was talking about. "You on your way to Winter Formal?"

"Nah. Hunter flaked on me so I'm solo dolo right now."

"What… that's crazy." Acting like I sympathized but I really didn't. Her loss. She stupid.

"You want to hang out or something since it seems like everyone else going to Winter Formal?"

I put my hand over the phone and told Melissa what Q just said. She goin' say she can't let me out because my daddy would flip. How he goin' know unless she tell him? I thought she was cool. My mood just went from 60-0 in like 1.5 milliseconds. *Whatever that means, but it sounds smart.* All this fly-ness going to waste because of stupid grownups. Ugh!

"Tell him to come over here instead." She whispered to me.

Hecks yeah! I take it back. She cooler than an air conditioner sitting in an igloo window in Alaska. I try to play it cool. "I don't know. I'm chilling at my dad's crib with his girlfriend right now while he's at work."

"Oh, aight… another time then."

Duh! Hello! Is he that dumb that he didn't catch that. I felt like this moment was about to flat line and I needed to get them electrical thingies to get the mood back alive. "You can come chill with us if you want. We just sitting here turnin' up."

"Oh, that's wassup! Turn down for what! Give me the address and I'll swoop through.

When he knocked on the door, I answered it and he goin' say, "Amber here?" I was like, "Boy quit playing." His eyes got huge as heck. He stepped in and grabbed my hand and twirled me around like we were hand dancing.

"Dang Ma! You lookin' real good!"

"Thanks, you lookin' real fly too!"

I introduced him to Melissa and told him she was my step-mom. She even let us go down into the basement by ourselves to give us some privacy. Now that's what I'm talkin' 'bout! Finally someone who respects me and understand that I'm old enough to have company and privacy. But she goin' say, 'No hanky-panky'. I don't even know what that is. I just said, okay.

But yeah, my dad got his basement set up real nice. It's like a bar down here. Not like, I knew what one really looked like, but I seen enough on TV.

Melissa said we could have a little of the Paul Mason but not to touch the Hennessey because that was daddy's and he'd know something was up.

I felt like I was having my own private Winter Formal. This was fine enough for me. Q asked me if it was okay if he lit up a joint he had. I told him, goin' head. I figured smoking cigarettes, and we drinking why not.

We took a few puffs and here comes Melissa running down the steps. "I know I don't smell what I think I smell!"

I mean dang! What she got against some bud? It was too late for Q to put it out cause Melissa was already standing right there. Quincy was sitting there stuck on stupid looking like he just was caught with his hands in the cookie jar.

"Oh, my bad. I'm sorry."

"Don't be sorry, pass that!" Melissa took a few puffs and started lighting incense and sitting them all around the basement.

I was beginning to feel like I was in a house unsupervised. Q had started to sing his rap song, "Son of a Battlefield" and he sounded good too! I didn't know he could be so deep. Q turned on some music and we was jammin' until my cell rang again. I wasn't about to pull out that ugly thing in front of Q and have him kicking it on me. I told them I'd be right back.

Niggas must can sense when a chick is looking fly because now it was Roman calling. "Hey bae!"

"Amber?"

"Yeah, dis me!" I tried to make my voice not slur too much but it was hard. "You at Winter Formal?"

"Nah, not yet." I could tell he was sounding a bit down.

"What's wrong?"

"Nothing. I don't even know why I called."

"Why don't you come by my dad's house real quick before you go to Winter Formal?"

I gave him the address and he got there in no time. I left Q and Melissa downstairs dancing, drinking, and smoking. They won't even know I'm gone. I'm not leaving though, just sitting in the car with Roman.

"Dang! You going to Winter Formal?" He asked me that cause I was doin' 'em and for the first time, I knew it.

"Not unless you taking me?" I was flirting the best I could. I looked at his tie and vest and it was a hot pink, humph… Symphony's dress must be pink too. "We already matching." I reached over and rubbed his waves.

He looked at me and laughed a little. "Not unless you want Symph, to kill us both."

Great another killjoy. Why can't people just play along and have some fun that way Quincy and I do. I know he's with Symphony… big deal.

I don't know if I'll ever get another chance like this again. I'm beautiful, my hair is long, my make-up is on point, my dress is the bomb.com, and I'm dang near wearing stilettos. No night can ever beat this. But the best part is, I'm sitting in Roman's car. The same seat that Symphony sat in. I knew I'd get here. It was only a matter of time. Who cares that he's about to go pick her up and take her to Winter Formal. He's here with me right now and she's at home… alone… waiting on him. I wanted to just reach over, grab his face, and kiss his juicy lips. That's just what I'm about to do.

"Roman?" He turns to look at me and I wiggle my index finger for him to come closer. He does and I chicken out and whisper in his ear. "I like you." He leans in closer and whispers in my ear, "I know."

Errrk! Scratch the record! In my mind, it's like I did a double take. He must don't understand so I did it. I grabbed his face with both of my hands and I put my lips on his. It wasn't no tongue action or nothing like that. More like a long peck. Well it seemed like an eternity to me but it was actually like three seconds. Don't laugh. Three seconds feels like forever. Put your hand over a fiery flame and see how long you last.

He broke away from me first. "Don't do that."

"Don't do what?"

"Don't be that girl."

He just don't know. I want to be that girl. All this is about me becoming that girl.

"You know I'm with Symphony. Plus you was just all over my boy the last time we were out. That's not a good look."

Who the hell he think he talking to. I do what I want. Forget him. I try to act like his comment didn't faze me none. "Then why are you here, Roman?"

"I'm here because I thought we were cool and you asked me too. Besides that, I was dealing with something and thought you could be someone I could talk to." He looks toward the front door but I don't take my eyes off him. "I thought you were different than all them other thotties out here, but you the same. Sorry to break it down to you, but you not my type. So I don't care how much make-up you put on, how long a weave, or how short a dress… you still not my type."

Before he stopped talking, I think I stopped hearing him speak. My world was crashing down all around me and exploded on impact. He fired insults at me as if his mouth was a .38 revolver, I was the target, and my heart was the bulls eye. We were at a shooting range. I'd have to say he was a great shot because everything that darted out of his mouth dang near killed me.

"Ro! Man, what you doing here? You trying to steal ma' girl?" Quincy was talking to Roman from the window where I sat.

"Nah bruh, she all yours. Sorry 'bout you and Hunter though."

"It's all good. It is what it is."

It took everything I had in me to not drop no tears. Only thing I was thinking about right now was running to my dude, Paul Mason. I wanted another drink, some more weed, and a cigarette or something. That's what I wanted. What I needed was a time machine so I could go back to before I tried to kiss him. I'm so stupid!

"Man, I just called you too."

Roman felt his body and checked his pockets. "Aw man, I left my phone on the charger at the crib. I need to bounce man… Symph goin' kill me."

Roman sat there looking at me. I know he was waiting for me to get out but I felt frozen… stiff… dead.

"C'mon baby. Get out this man's car so he can go get his wifey."

As soon as I open Roman's car door, Quincy pushes me out of the way and sits in the passenger's seat. "Hold up, turn that up bruh! They announcing the winners of the contest!"

"You sure you want to torture yourself like that man?" Roman asked but Quincy ignored his question and turns up the volume himself.

'WELL, IT'S THAT MOMENT YOU'VE ALL BEEN WAITING FOR. THE WINNERS WILL RECEIVE $5000 AND A ONE SONG RECORDING DEAL WITH GIMMIE SUM DAP RECORDS!'

"Damn man…" Quincy looked at Roman. "That could have been me… well us." He smiled a little and put his head down. I knew he was feeling bad by what all had went down.

'AND THE WINNERS ARE… 'SON OF A BATTLEFIELD' BY REMY AND PATRÓN WALKER!'

"Wait, Quincy ain't that your song?" He was just downstairs talking about that song. I see Quincy and Roman sit straight up and jerk as if they had been electrocuted. Quincy cupped his chin with his hand. His face was so wrinkled it was as if he was smelling something real bad. Roman on the other hand, his mouth was just hanging wide open but nothing was coming out.

"What the!" Q yells at the radio and then looks at Roman. "That's my song!"

Lyrics pour from the car speakers like arrows plunging into Quincy's body like an old school execution. I felt his pain and understood his anger. His head turns slowly towards Roman. "How they get my demo, man?"

Roman sat there in silence.

"How they get my freakin' demo, Roman?"

"I-I don't know, Q." I don't know about Q, but I had a feeling that Roman was not being truthful. He just seemed too scared or something.

"Nigga! Don't give me that! You know something! They got your exact beat and my exact lyrics!" Veins popped out of every place that Q had veins and spit began to fly out of his mouth with each word. "Them bastards didn't even have the audacity to change the freakin' song title!" Quincy pounded his fist with each word. "You played me Ro! I don't know how or why. You had me thinking you gave a damn that day. Had me running and humiliating myself and for what, nigga?" I try to grab Q by the arm and pull him out of the car because things were getting heated real fast. I look over at Roman and all I see are tears streaming down his face but no sound.

"You always gotta outshine me! Ain't it enough you got football, nigga?" Just that quick Quincy reaches over and start to punch Roman in the face. I'm yelling, screaming, and falling, dang near breaking my ankle trying to stop these two from killing each other. I ain't goin' lie, I did hesitate for a minute. Serves him right to take a few punches to the face the way he was just treating me a few minutes ago.

"Quincy, please!" I grab the back of Q's shirt and pull. He finally stops. "Let's just go back into the house, Q."

"What's going on out here?" Melissa comes running outside.

A few of Quincy's buttons came loose and his shirt was totally untucked and wrinkled. But it didn't matter to me because seeing him beat on Roman like that had me make-believing that they were fighting over me. *What? A girl can dream can't she? Or are you being a killjoy like, Willow?*

30 CHAPTER THIRTY
SYMPHONY PERKINS

When you really matter to someone, that person will always make time for you. No excuses, no lies, and no broken promises.

I CHECKED THE TIME again. Oh hell no! It's only like an hour and a half of Winter Formal left. This nigga ain't even answering my calls. That is one thing I don't play. I called Jaylen and Q but they claimed they ain't heard from him either. Ooooh! I can't believe he goin' play me like that.

I looked at myself one last time in my full-length mirror. I can't believe all this went to waste. My dress was a hot pink ball gown and the bustier was zebra print. It took me a while to gather all the materials I needed and put the one of a kind masterpiece together. I guess I just wasted my time making two gorgeous dresses. Hunter's and mine.

Karma is definitely a biatch! I guess I shouldn't have been talking about her when she said she couldn't go to Winter Formal. O well, I'll either store this up for next year or sell it on eBay. One way or another, it's going to get some use. And I will let Hunter know that she giving me back my dress.

I had my own photo-shoot by myself. I was thinking about posting them to Facebook but then I decided against it. I didn't want to get bombarded with questions about where I was, or how come I didn't go. Plus, people would know if I do decide to wear it next year.

I reached behind my back *because I'm double jointed like that* and unzipped my own zipper. I let my dress fall to the floor. I stand there for a moment staring at my two-piece pink and zebra striped laced undies. I sashayed a bit, looking at myself from each angle. His loss.

I called Roman again just to give him the common courtesy he wasn't mature enough to give me…

AT THIS POINT IDGAF WHAT U DOIN OR WHAT HAPPENED. IM THROUGH W/ UR CORNY SELF… DON'T BOTHER 2 CALL BACK OR COME BY… I HOPE U WRECK UR GMA'S BEATER & GET HURT SO BAD U HAVE TO SIT OUT THE REST OF THE SEASON. KMMFA NIGGA! I GOTTA MAN & HE AIN'T U!!!!

I kicked my dress into the corner and laid down on my bed. I rumble through my purse until I found DeKing's number. I twirl the card with my fingers wondering if I should even bother. I was bored and didn't feel like talking to Hunter. I knew Spirit and Jaylen was already knee-deep into Winter Formal. I guess I had no choice but to call him.

He answers the phone right away and I knew it was him. "May I speak to 'The King'?"

He laughs and says, "Who's speaking?"

That rather annoyed me because now I'm wondering how many women does he meet or deal with. But then again, we did just meet and he is an older guy. At least I think he is. "This is—"

"I know. How are you Symphony?"

Wow, impressive, he did remember me. But then again, who wouldn't… "I'm fine and you?"

"Oh, I can't complain. So what are you getting into this evening?"

Well I sure couldn't tell him where I had originally planned to go or else he'd know I was still in high school. "Nothing."

"Nothing? Well, do you want to do something?"

"Something like what?"

"I don't know what do you like to do?"

I was stumped. I never had to answer that question before. "A lot of things I guess. Going out to eat… to the movies… bowling."

"Really?"

"Yeah… I guess."

"That's text book dating. Everyone goes out to eat, movies, and bowling. That's like saying, "I love long walks in the park…" I'm sure that's a cliché on all those dating sites." He laughs but I'm wondering what he's doing on dating sites. He clears his throat. "Okay, let me rephrase the question. What would you like to do but have never done?"

Y'all thought I was stumped on the first question, I was really stumped now. The farthest I ever went in my thinking was for Roman to take me to the movies on time. "Slow down DeKing… you asking me all these questions and I don't even know how long you've been on this earth." That was my way of diverting the question.

"Are you asking me for my age?" Hmmmph… his voice was so dang sexy!

"Positive." I grab my laptop and log onto Facebook to see if I could secretly see if he had a Facebook page.

"Does age matter?" Hold up, why he don't want to answer how old he is? "I'm asking because that's such a routine question when you meet someone before dating… as if people will fall in love with the number and not the person."

"True. But you have to ask these days because people have gone to jail getting caught up with those they thought weren't minor."

"Well, as long as you're not a minor, we should be in the clear, right?"

"Do you not want to answer my question?" Again my way of diverting having to lie.

"I'm messing with you baby, I'm twenty-three."

Daaaaaang!!! My mouth flew wide open and wouldn't close. I shut the top down on my laptop and didn't even finish searching for him. I didn't know whether to hang up the phone or act more mature. Unfortunately, I chose the latter. At this point, the only thing for me to do was ask, "Do you have any kids?"

"No. No kids. But I do know you have a little girl right?" We both laughed because I now knew he was joking. "So, back to the matter at hand. Do you want to go out tonight? If it would make you more comfortable, maybe we can meet up for drinks at Charlie's. Do you drink?"

He was asking so many questions because again, my mouth was open and nothing came out. How was I going to get out of this? I'm only 16! I drink, but not legally. "Yes, I drink a little here and there but I'm not really the bar or club scene type of chick. I'm more of a laid-back-stay-at-home and chill kind of female.

"Great answer. Most girls your age like to live in the club drinking and partying every weekend.

"Wait. Great answer?" I mimicked him. "Was that supposed to be a test question?"

"Isn't all pre-dating questions?"

"You said, girls my age. I haven't told you my age yet."

"We already established we weren't minors, right?"

We talked a little while longer getting to know each other. He invited me over to his house for some take-out. Normally I would insist on the guy coming to get me because I don't do deliveries. But in this case the boy was a man and I had to make sure I liked him first before he found out where I lived. I would have waited maybe a few more weeks before I went to his house but this was a special occasion since Roman stood me up. He still hasn't called.

31 CHAPTER THIRTY-ONE

Winter Formal

THE WINTER FORMAL DANCE was poppin' and everyone were enjoying themselves. Jaylen and Spirit stayed on the dance floor. Jaylen especially loved slow dancing with Spirit. It was the most action he'd gotten from her since they had started dating years ago.

Willow and Ryder had come together as each other's dates. They'd dance to a few of their favorite fast songs but sat out on all the slow ones.

"I-It's messed up th-th-that Amber couldn't come. I know she was really lo-looking f-forward to Winter…Formal."

"Ryder please… I'm about done feeling sorry for Amber. She gets what she deserves."

"Th-that's mean."

"Maybe a little. She's probably glad she's on punishment because she couldn't find a date. I wouldn't put it past her if she got on punishment on purpose to have an excuse."

Willow and Ryder grabbed some punch that was already poured into cups sitting on the punch table.

"I-I still can't b-believe she snuck out?"

"I can't believe she lied and fantasized about Roman liking her."

"W-why you so-so hard on her?" Ryder took a sip of his punch and waited for Willow to respond.

"I'm not hard on her!" Willow glared at Ryder and scanned the room with her eyes. "I wonder where her little squad is. The only ones I see here is Spirit and Jaylen, but they don't really hang with them anyway."

"W-why you-you checking for 'the squad'? I h-had a chance to h-hang with them and they w-weren't that bad." She walked away and left Ryder standing there.

♥♥♥

"Aren't you tired of dancing?" Spirit asked Jaylen as they swayed to another slow jam. "My feet are starting to hurt in these shoes."

"Nope." He pulls her in closer and lays her head closer to his heart.

"Hold up." Spirit reaches down and removes her heels. Jaylen, being the gentleman that he is, grabs them and hold them for her and they both continue slow dancing. "I wonder where everyone is?"

"Well, Hunter and Q broke up, so I guess they're not coming. And I don't really know where Symphony and Roman are. He's probably somewhere heated because we got into it."

"Who got into it? You and Roman?" They stop dancing and Spirit drags Jaylen to a little more quieter place to talk.

"It's not even that serious Spirit." Jaylen didn't want to talk about it. "You know how heated Roman gets over nothing."

"Well, tell me the nothing he got upset about? What happened?"

"I don't know." Jaylen began to pace back and forth. "He came back home to get his cell off the charger. He acted stupid. We fought. He took my grandma's car. He left. That was it. He's probably with Symphony and she decided to just babysit him."

"Hmm… that don't sound right." Spirit grabs her cell from her purse and calls Symphony. No answer so she leaves Symphony a message to call her. "You call Roman."

"No."

"Why?"

"I'm not talking to that dude. Period. He can die as far as I'm concerned!"

"You're not supposed to say things like that, Jaylen! Take it back!"

"No!"

"What could he have done to you that was so bad it got you wishing death on somebody?"

♥♥♥

"I'm going to stay right here in the parking lot. Your dad gets off at midnight, so we have to be home well before then."

What else was new! Classic Cinderella story. Amber thought as she and Quincy got out of Melissa's car and headed inside of Westbrook High. The plan was to walk into Winter Formal, say hello to a few people so Amber could floss, and have one slow dance with Quincy. He told Amber that she at least deserved that. To go to her first Winter Formal and have at least one dance. The two however, convinced Melissa to take them and she agreed, as long as it was the three's secret.

"Oowee! I got the hottest date in Westbrook!" Quincy yelled as he handed the ticket handlers two tickets. One of them originally meant for Hunter. He kissed Amber on the cheek and grabbed her by the waist as he led her into the gym.

"Wait!" Amber stopped dead in her tracks

"What? You ain't getting cold feet are you?"

"Never that! I just need to go to the ladies room. That's all. Wait for me."

"Oh, I ain't going nowhere bae." Amber's heart fluttered from Quincy's soft tone and word choice.

She couldn't believe that she was finally here at Winter Formal, with a date, and looking fly as ever. She click clacked her heels, (well, Melissa's heels but she was owning them tonight) and sashayed her rear because she knew Quincy was looking. To her, it was all a dream. Forget Roman's ugly self. Maybe he ain't my type! She thought about the comment that Roman said before he left her father's house. Those words he said to her cut her deeply. She felt that hurt all through her soul. He talking 'bout don't be that chick. Humph! "*I am that bitch*!" She said aloud to herself in the mirror as she fixed the bangs on her wig.

"Omygosh! Amber?" Willow came out of the bathroom stall and washed her hands as her mouth hung open the whole time.

Amber however, had forgotten all about Willow being at Winter Formal. "There go your snitchin' self!"

"I can't believe your mom let you come! And dressed like that!"

"What you mean, dressed like that?" Amber was already mad and getting madder. Every time she makes a come up on something, someone always has to ruin it for her. Amber refused to let anyone take this night from her. It was her time to shine and she was going to shine brighter than any star in the sky. She might not have been with Roman, but Quincy was the next best thing.

Thoughts of Roman's words floated in her head again mixed with Willow's words of how Roman didn't really like her. Right now, all Amber felt was hatred. Amber wiped the water sprinkles off the countertop with a paper towel. "You know what, Willow?" Amber carefully removed her wig, placed it neatly on the counter, and removed Melissa's four-inch fuchsia heels. She walked over to Willow and eased her fingers through Willow's immaculately decorated bun.

"Amber. Stop. What are you doing?"

"I hate you!" Amber pulled Willow's bun a loose as she yanked on her hair and began to punch willow in the face repeatedly. Even though it was Willow's face that was taking all the abuse, inside Amber was pummeling Roman as well.

"Stop!" Willow cried. "I'm tellin'!"

This just added more fuel to the fire. "That's all you ever do is tell!"

Amber hit Willow a few more times before she slung Willow to the floor dirtying up her canary yellow ball gown. Willow sat there on the floor stunned about what just took place. She held her face in her hands and sobbed. She could feel the knots forming on her forehead and cheekbones.

Willow looked up at Amber placing the wig back on her head and fixing her way to short dress. "You're just jealous." Willow said in between sobs.

Amber adjusted her breast and blew a kiss into the mirror. "No boo! Not today!"

Willow looked down at the bloodstains covering her formal dress. She reached up and snatched a paper towel to stop the blood from pouring from her nose. "You're crazy!" She grabbed her cellphone and began to scroll through to find her mother's number. "Wait until I tell my mom! You think you're on punishment now!"

Amber ran up to Willow, grabbed her cell phone away from her, and hurled it to the floor. She took her heel and crushed the screen into pieces. "Runtelldat! Snitch!" Amber ran back into the hallway to find Quincy so she could have her one dance. Instead, Quincy comes running up behind her with Jaylen and Spirit tailing behind him.

"C'mon… we gotta go!"

"Go where?"

"Jaylen just got a call from his grandma, said Roman has been in a bad accident. You think Melissa can drop us off at the hospital?"

32 CHAPTER THIRTY-TWO

I just want you that's it. All your flaws, mistakes, smiles, giggles, jokes, sarcasm. Everything. I just want you.

SYMPHONY AND DEKING WERE in the middle of eating and engrossed in conversation when her cell kept blowing up. She would sit there and monitor her phone screening calls just in case her mother called and needed her car back. However, she refused to take any calls from anyone who attended Westbrook High. She wasn't in the mood to hear how things were going at a homecoming that she was stood up for. Besides, tonight she was on her grown woman thang, Symphony did not have time for little kids tonight.

"Someone must be really trying to get a hold of you. Boyfriend?" DeKing asked as he wiped his mouth with a napkin.

Symphony rolls her eyes annoyed by the many callers plaguing her phone. "Oh, it's my mother, I'd better take this."

"Hello, Mother."

"Symphony?"

"What's wrong?"

"It's… It's Roman honey." Symphony got up and excused herself to the bathroom. "I don't what to hear nothing about Roman and his many excuses. He can roll over and die for all I care!"

"Baby, he—he's been in a bad car accident."

"Are you kidding me? How bad?"

"I don't know. Evelyn called and told me. She doesn't even know yet. They took him straight back to surgery."

"Oh my God! Mom." Symphony fought back the tears as hard as she could but some still escaped and fell down her cheeks staining her foundation. "I gotta go."

Symphony hung up with her mother and ran out on DeKing without giving him much information except that a friend was hurt badly and she needed to get to the hospital. It was hard for her to drive because she was crying so hard. Her legs were shaking uncontrollably that for a minute she thought she was going to have to pull over on the side of the road until she got a grip of herself.

♥♥♥

At the hospital, the first person that Symphony ran to was Evelyn. "How is he?"

"Chile, we don't know. We don't know nothing about nothing and they ain't' telling us nothing. All we know is that when they brought him in here, he was unconscious."

"Girl, where you been? I've been trying to get a hold of you for the longest!" Symphony wasn't in the mood for Spirit's nosey self-right now. She waved Spirit off and went to go hug Jaylen, who was sitting there with major attitude.

"Hey, J?" He just nodded his head as a greeting.

"Where the hell was you at Symphony?" Quincy was sitting next to Amber and Melissa.

"None of your dayum business Quincy! You ain't nobody's daddy!"

"Well, obviously you weren't with Roman. You was probably somewhere boppin' it up with some nigga, ya *THOT!*. Prolly reason why ma-man laying up in here now."

Symphony leaped over Hunter and the baby and went straight for Quincy's head. "I got yo THOT… ya MAN-THOT!" Evelyn jumped up before Symphony made contact. "Y'all stop all this damn bickering! I'm old. My grandson in surgery. I don't even know if he dead or not and y'all carrying on like dis! Stop it. Stop it now!"

Everyone got quiet all of a sudden. So quiet you could hear a pin drop. After ten minutes of quiet, Hunter couldn't take looking at Quincy and Amber. She couldn't hold her silence in any longer. "I see it didn't take you long to move on?"

"What? You thought it would?" Quincy leaned over and put his arms around Amber.

Symphony chuckled to herself a bit, "C'mon now Hunter, stop. You're sounding a lil thirsty boo!" She was being sarcastic reminiscing about the bus ride when Amber sat with Roman.

"Excuse me?" Hunter looked at Symphony while bouncing Josiah on her knee.

"Karma Boo. Karma… that's all I'm going to say. Besides, I told you about those two and all you did was hand him to her. On a silver platter with a cherry on top. Symphony popped her lips to make a popping sound.

"You make it sound like I'm pressed. Have you ever thought that maybe it was my plan to get rid of Q to make room for my new man?"

"Boo please, what new man? You don't go nowhere or do nothing anyway without a baby attached to your hip like you're its mother. Ooh... how sexy is that!"

Hunter wanted so bad to tell her the truth because obviously Roman hadn't yet. She wanted to sit Josiah on Symphony's lap and say Boo that Bitch! You're holding Roman and mines baby. But she didn't. She didn't say not one word. She felt bad enough that Roman had gotten into the car accident because of her. She kept replaying over and over in her mind her version of the events she thought took place regarding Roman's accident. She pictures him driving and then reaching for his cell to check his messages and when he gets to hers. BAM! He loses all control when he finds out that he fathered her baby. Hunter sits and eyes everyone in the squad wondering if Roman had told anyone anything.

Symphony sits and falls into deep thought. I shouldn't have sent that message! I did this. This is my fault. If I hadn't wished he'd get into an accident and die, none of this would have happened. Maybe, I wouldn't have even hooked up with DeKing. Maybe Roman and I would have gone to Homecoming and had a great time and kicked it like we usually do. I can't believe how selfish I was. There I was sitting there heated because he was late picking me up. No wonder he was late! He was smashed up somewhere probably dying while I was out wining and dining with some random dude. Maybe Q was right.

"Get yo behind up and move... right now!" Symphony was startled out of her thoughts wondering who this lady was yelling at until she saw Amber roll her eyes and stand up.

"Ma! I'm not leaving until I find out if my friend is okay."

"Friend? Since when did you have any friends other than Ryder and Willow? Whom you viciously pounded half to death in a place you weren't supposed to even be!"

"Ma! You're embarrassing me." Amber clutched her teeth as she spoke.

"Well, how do you think Willow felt?" Joi stepped closer to her daughter. "What is this mess you have on? Whose stuff is this?" She eyed the teenaged girls looking for someone to fess up.

"It's... It's mine." As Melissa stood up Russell held his head in shame and embarrassment.

Joi looked at her ex-husband, then to Melissa, and back at Amber's feet. "Take it off! Joi snatched the wig from Amber's head and the shoes from her feet and threw them at Melissa. "If you ever... play dress up with my daughter and have her looking like a hoe, I will kill you my damn self!"

"Yo… lady, no disrespect but—"Quincy was referring to Amber's mother.

"Sit you butt down boy and stay out of people's business." Evelyn chimed and Quincy obeyed.

Amber sat in the chair with her face in her hands the whole time crying her eyes out. Symphony pulled some tissue from her bag and handed it to Amber. "Rule #3."

Amber tried her best to stop crying as Russell wrestled Joi out the door and into the parking lot. When the surgeon had finally come out, everyone got quiet and stood at attention. "As of right now, we've done all that we could do. It was a little touch and go, but he's stable."

"Oh thank God!" Evelyn collapsed in her seat as she held her heart and continued to listen.

"At this point I don't want you to get your hopes up. He has some swelling of the brain… so he has a concussion and a few broken bones. One of his broken ribs punctured his lung and it collapsed." Everyone gasped at the thought of Roman going through all that. They all held each other as if no one had any problems with the other. "We will keep you posted on his condition and let you know when you can go back."

"So what does that mean?" Symphony wanted to know. "He hasn't really told us anything!"

"Well, we know he ain't dead! That's good enough for me right now. We just have to keep praying."

Everyone breathed a sigh of relief and Melissa and Amber began to walk out to the parking lot. "Hold up." Quincy ran to catch up to Amber. "Can I just talk to her for like a quick second?" Quincy said to Melissa.

"If I were you I'd make it quick." She looked at Amber. "I'm going to head out and see where your dad is. Don't stay to long, alright babygirl?"

Amber kept her head down because she felt she had been stripped of any confidence or dignity she had. Her hair was a mess and stood all over her head. Her makeup was smeared from breaking rule #3, and her feet were cold from being barefoot.

"C'mon bae." Quincy hugged Amber and rubbed her back. "That shit was foul that yo moms did to you."

"I hate her! I'm so embarrassed right now."

"Don't be, baby." Quincy held Amber's face and kissed her on the forehead and then on the lips. "You got my number right." Amber nodded her head yes. "Use that. I don't care what time it is or even if you don't even really want nothing. Just use it, baby okay?"

Amber cracked a smile and looked up into Quincy's eyes and for that moment, she felt as if she loved him. She didn't care that she was probably about to get her butt beat when she got home. This was enough to cover a multitude of anything thing she was about to face. She really wanted to hug him so tight and tell him she loved him, but even she knew that would be a dummy move.

"Amber! Now!" Russell stuck his head inside the doors and called his daughter. Amber however, rolled her eyes to the ceiling.

"Do you see what I have to deal with?"

"Yeah, you parents bugged out. Just try to play it cool though so you don't be on punishment too long."

"Alright." Amber began to blush.

"I'ma miss you baby. That is until I see you in school, right?"

Amber nodded her head and went home with her mother to suffer any consequences she had. She was placed on strict lock down and because of Quincy's love and pep talk, she was able to do it all without talking back. She was on cloud nine for weeks and even though she never got that dance, visions of Quincy's kiss danced in her head forever.

Fitting in is unnecessary. Embrace who you are. You will go through rough times in high school, but always stay strong, and never deny yourself!
~Neon Hitch

Thanks so much for reading, I hope you enjoyed it. Stay tuned for Semester II coming soon!

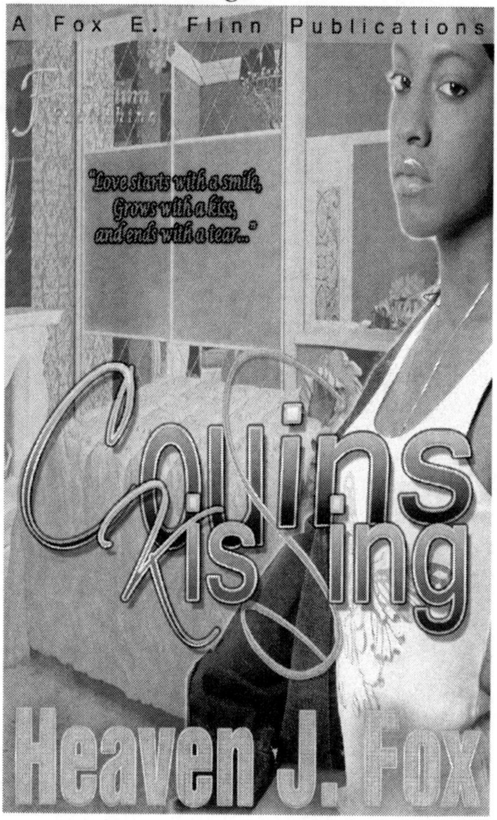

Also for a short story be sure to check out Kissing Cousins on Amazon.